The Marvelous Invention of Orion McBride

TO THE KIDS WHO ARE
CARRYING MORE THAN THEY
SHOULD HAVE TO.

Edited by Claire Evans and Chris Rogers
Cover and book design by David Miles

Cover and decorative graphics licensed from Shutterstock.com.

ISBN 978-1-7360770-0-9 (paperback)

ISBN 978-1-7360770-1-6 (e-book)

The Marvelous Invention of Orion McBride

TYLER ROGERS

Contents

PART 1

The Magician

CHAPTER 1

Teleport

I'VE NEVER WONDERED BEFORE ABOUT HOW hard I would need to throw a baseball to break a window. It's tempting me now, though. The red stitching of Dad's signature Mariners ball feels smooth under my thumb, and I think about what raining glass might sound like as it hits a cold wooden floor.

Makes me think of a new plot idea: *Boy shatters the whole world with one throw.*

I try to toss the ball as high as I can without hitting the ceiling. I fail. I try to go three seconds without thinking of Dad. I fail.

Rhythmic taps on my door are followed by Mom's voice.

"Hiya, Critter," she says. "Getting all settled in?" Her face gets real heavy when she sees the same skyline of unopened boxes lining the walls of my still-empty bedroom. Six hours and nothing's changed. It's well past lunch time now.

She notices the book on my bed. *Year of The Dreamer.* I picked it up when we went to the library this morning. I pretended to browse books while Mom and that white-haired librarian lady talked about what to do with me after school like I was some troublesome burden. I settled on *Year of The Dreamer* because it was the lone title on the Book of the Day display, so it seemed special. That, and it was close enough to Mom for me to eavesdrop. I told Mom that I would unpack after I read for a while. Truth is that I haven't even read the first page. I know a lie when I say one.

"Do you want any help? Oakley and I are almost done with her room."

I look anywhere but at her and shake my head no. "Maybe later," I say. I hold up the ball. "I just want some think time."

"Okay," she says as she nods in understanding. She rests her head on the door frame and looks at me for a long moment. I know exactly what she is going to do next. She's going to pull out her phone from her left side pocket and take a picture of me. And it goes just like that, but I don't look at the camera. It makes me want to scream. I think about being a pitcher for the Seattle Mariners and blasting the phone out of her hands with the baseball. Wind up. *Blam.* Impeccable accuracy. The crowd roars its approval.

"It's going to be special here, too," Mom says softly, smearing away my daydream. "I love you."

I start to play catch with myself and imagine setting a world record for the most tosses and catches in a row. But my catch streak ends at nine and I watch the ball roll away to a corner. Too far. Just another thing that is *too far*.

Dad was going to take me to a Seattle Mariners baseball game this summer. I don't give even a tiny care about baseball. Or about any sports, really. But now that Dad is gone, summer might as well not even come this year. Just cancel it.

Plot idea: *Boy teleports planet forward in its orbit.*

I try to shrink away into the navy-blue weave of my hoodie. It's the Mariners one. It just has a warmth to it. That, and Mom says the rich color compliments my light hair.

I have permission to design my new bedroom any way I want to, probably because it's one less thing for Mom to have to sort out. She's made a mess of enough already. I try to imagine where I might put my books. My art supplies. My writing desk with its folders of unfinished stories and illustrations. But I shake all of those thoughts away when I see Dad's baseball at the door. I'm not interested in getting too comfortable here. I have no intention of being a longtime resident on Willoughby Lane. I just want to go home. Dad and I have plans for the summer.

CHAPTER 2

Shorts

I SLIP ON MY TENNIS SHOES WITHOUT DOING THE laces. Mom hates when I do that. I can hear Disney music blaring out from Oakley's new room on the opposite side of the house. And it makes my brain go backwards like it's been doing a lot lately.

It takes me back home to Oregon. I remember how I had side-by-side rooms with my sister. We'd created a system of more than ten wall-tap signals. Two taps was an invitation to play. Four taps was a warning that Mom or Dad was grumpy. It made us feel like detectives. We even made a picture book about it. I did the words and Oakley did the pictures. Scribbly, scratchy crayon bending the paper. But we stopped doing things like that when Dad pled guilty. Everything stopped when Dad pled guilty.

"Chris!" Oakley says when she sees me peeking through the cracked open door of her new bedroom. "Chris look!"

She draws both arms out in a regal way in front of the built-in shelving, underlining the many rows of her stuffed animal legion, several that she's had since before she could walk. If Oakley were a storybook character, she'd be royal commander of all things soft and fluffy. She'd oversee ranks and ranks of stuffed companions. Whatever the opposite of an iron fist is, that's what she would rule with. Of course, Stardust is front and center in Oakley's toy display.

Stardust is a royal blue stuffed rabbit that Dad gave Oakley after her appendix surgery when she was in kindergarten. The rabbit is a regular guest at dinner time and is basically another member of the family. I remember Oakley getting regularly scolded by Dad for taking Stardust to school. Well, back at the old school. I tried to tell her that second graders are too old to bring toys to class, but she would just stick her tongue out.

"What do you think, Critter?" Mom asks. Oakley's room has been set up in almost the exact same way it was back in Oregon. Bed in the corner, desk by the window, toy chest just left of the closet door.

"And Mom said that we can paint all the walls green!" Oakley says, punctuating the word *green* with a clap.

It frustrates me to see Oakley smiling. Just the other night we sat in our empty Oregon living room and I didn't know that one little girl could be full of so many tears. But now it's like she forgot all of that. It's like she's forgotten about Dad. She's giddy and seeing her smile makes me feel like I have a bloody nose. Mom sneaks a picture of Oakley as she adjusts the spacing of her toy empire, shifting her weight back and forth.

"I'm going for a walk," I say. Mom reminds me to be safe and I leave the house to the tune of my sister shrieking her best version of a singing princess.

It only takes thirty seconds for me to regret not wearing a bigger coat. The January air pierces straight through my Mariners hoodie. I've never known wind to be so vicious.

Plot idea: *Lost boy tames the polar wind, rides it back to his homeland.*

Mom told us to expect cold and snow when we moved here. She was right about the cold. But the snow? A total swing and miss.

I stand in the middle of the road and look all the way down Willoughby Lane, our new street. It's a flat and tiny side-street neighborhood tucked neatly in the residential grid of Cortland, Wyoming. It's quiet. Like, I can't even hear birds or cars sorts of quiet. Three blocks one way is Weston Elementary. Two blocks the other way is the library with a distant mountain scape rolling on behind it. In between is just weathered houses, asphalt, and dead grass. If there was a world record for the most bleak and dreary town ever, Cortland would easily be a contender.

I spot a neon green bike abandoned in the yard next to mine. Makes me wonder if maybe there are other kids here on Willoughby Lane. Oakley and I used to go on hour-long bike rides with Dad. He was so proud and surprised when I taught Oakley how to ride. We all grabbed helmets and rode all the way to the ice cream shop. The cookie dough was extra sweet that day.

I sit down in the middle of Willoughby Lane. Being cold beats being inside right now. Mom would flip if she saw me sitting in the middle of the road, but these streets aren't like Oregon streets. They're motionless here. Still, it makes me think about what it might be like to have telekinetic powers. The ability to stop a car zooming at full speed with the slightest push of my hand. But the wintry silence and my story building is broken to pieces by a shout.

"Christopher!" Someone yells. It's an unfamiliar young voice. They shout my name a second time. It's coming from the front door of my neighbor's house. The green bike house. A boy is running at me, full sprint. I look around in a panic, thinking that somebody else with my name must be nearby. When I meet his eyes again, I have just enough time to catch a wild blur of blue shorts and a golden yellow scarf as the wind gets knocked out of me and I am tackled to the ground.

CHAPTER 3

Orion

MOM SAYS THAT OAKLEY AND I ARE OPPO-
sites in every sense of the word. "Oakley is full
of motion. Chris is full of words," I once heard her say.
Back in fourth grade, there was another Chris in my class.
I became *Quiet Chris* and he became *Chatty Chris*. And
it wasn't because I had nothing to say. It's just that I often
don't know how to say what I am thinking. The words don't
line up for me very easily. And in this moment—being
pinned down in the middle of the street by a stranger kid
in a new town—my well of words has dried up completely.

I use two hands to push the boy off me and he rolls onto
his back. He's light. I have no idea how to fight somebody.
I try to recall fight scenes from the stories I've read, but
none come to mind fast enough. I leap up and raise my
fists in anticipation, but his face looks, to my surprise,
playful.

"Hi!" he says, dragging the word out for an hour with a raspy, high-pitched voice. He looks to be around my age. "Welcome back! I've missed you." He stands up and holds his hand out for a high five, but I leave him hanging. I look blankly at his open hand so he knows I'm doing it on purpose.

"That hurt," I say, rubbing my back where it met the asphalt.

"My bad," he says. "I didn't mean to hurt you. Honest." He talks quickly and expressively. Eyes wide. "You're back! It's literally you! How was the leap?" His freckly cheeks beam in the afternoon daylight, and his scarf bounces in the wind along with his light brown bangs.

I pray that Mom will come storming out of the house to scold me for being so mindless as to sit in the street. But it doesn't happen. "You have me confused for somebody else," I say. "I just moved here."

"Oh, stop," he says dramatically. He stands a few inches shorter than me. "I've been waiting *forever* for you to get back. We're gonna get it right this time," he says as he pounds one fist in an open hand. "Let's go!"

He brushes dirt off his legs, then pats the road crumbs off of my arms as well. The hamster in my brain is sprinting in its wheel trying to connect a memory to this boy. I look him up and down and up again. Not a familiar face from Oregon. And I haven't met a single person here in Cortland yet.

Plot idea: *Boy mistaken for a friend.*

"I've gotta go," I say.

His smile crumples I walk straight past him for my front door. I'm more than a little bothered that this shorts-wearing lunatic is apparently my next-door neighbor. I don't want random roadside tackling to be a thing I have to worry about on Willoughby Lane. Makes my brain flicker to think of everything else I have to worry about.

"Christopher Fritz, stop!" he says. I turn to stone, unintentionally obedient. Hearing my full name is jarring. How does he know it?

He gets in front of me and puts his hands on my shoulders. "It's me. Orion. Orion McBride? Hello?" He shakes me lightly.

"How do you know my name?" I ask.

Plot idea: *Boy mistaken for a stranger.*

He looks straight into me with strong eyes. "You really don't remember me, do you?" Orion tightens his fingers on my shoulders. I don't answer him. "Christopher Fritz, you have to trust me." He talks in a slow whisper. Even the wind pauses to give Orion room to speak. "I know this isn't your home. I can get you back."

CHAPTER 4

Lightning

IT ONLY TAKES ME ABOUT THIRTY SECONDS TO make a mess of pretty much all of Mom's safety rules. Sitting in the road, talking to a stranger, going into the house of said stranger. I wonder if this might be step one of something sinister, like a kidnapping or worse. God's probably shaking his head at me, preparing my ride up. But Orion seems especially non-suspicious. He looks like he is straight out of a preschool cartoon. Sky blue shorts, blazing red shirt, golden scarf, and a busy, bouncy body. *He seems harmless,* I think.

The wooden steps leading up to his front door squeak under my feet, and Orion turns around to give me the *shhh* sign with one finger. "Take your shoes off and carry them," he says as he slowly opens his front door and guides me inside. Odd instructions, but he does the same and a ripping sound reveals that his shoes have straps instead of laces.

"Velcro?" I ask.

"They're *self-fastening*. Efficiency matters, Christopher Fritz!" he answers. He's definitely harmless.

Orion moves soundlessly over an ocean of grey carpet. His words are repeating over and over in my head. *"I can get you back."* My brain is more curious about Orion than it is disappointed in me for sneaking into a house with a stranger kid. I follow his swift lead past several closed doors to a narrow staircase. Twelve steep steps bring us to a lonely wooden door and I nearly go blind when Orion opens it.

Plot idea: *Boy falls face first into a rainbow.*

Oakley would swoon. Sunbeams dance from a skylight onto a mosaic of person-sized triangles on the wall, colors clashing and colliding every which way. The covers on the bed, the rug, and cubby-like shelving are all splattered with squiggles and stripes. A big purple bean bag chair sits invitingly under a wacky lamp with several branching lights. Everything is rainbow but shaded slightly blue by a restaurant-size fish tank that hums softly. If I were to trip and land in a kindergarten coloring book, I would expect it to look something like this. Outside, Orion's colorful outfit had been a bit blinding. Here, he pretty much blends in.

Orion leaps into a chair at a computer and begins to click furiously. Mom says that I'm not old enough to have my own device. "You'd never leave the house, Critter, and you know it." A drop of envy swirls in me. I notice that he has a single book on display on a nightstand: *The Little Prince.*

Orion leaps back down to a swirly rug that reminds me of Saturn. He pats the floor for me to join. "Welcome back!" he says, still whispering.

"What do you mean *back?*" I ask, joining him on the rug. "You keep saying that."

"Duh!" Orion chirps. "We're time travelers!"

Plot idea: *Boys mistakes tattered parchment for treasure map; the journey has been for naught.*

"Time travel isn't real," I say, feeling both annoyed and embarrassed that I let myself get pulled into this kid's playscape.

"Don't be stupid, Christopher Fritz," he whispers back. "We're literally the first two people in the history of people to go back in time!" Orion's excitement is radiating. There is a frosty intensity in his eyes. Mom would say that he's got a pack of wild horses behind those eyes, and I think she'd be right.

"There's no such thing," I say. I think about the books I've read that have time travel. They're always in the fiction section.

"You literally don't remember the pictures? The missions? The leap?" He points to a bulletin board over his computer that is overfilled with small square-shaped photos. There are dozens of little squares. I can see Orion's face in many of them. Some pictures don't have people at all. Just things. A street sign. A flower. There's a girl with a backwards baseball cap in a lot of the pictures on the left side. "Fine. Let me explain."

Reluctantly, I let him.

Orion tells me that his father is a scientist who has spent his whole life researching something called *leaping.* "My father believes that leaping forward in time is likely an impossibility," he explains. "But leaping backwards is something we are nearly ready to do."

I pretend to be interested as Orion tells me *I* had helped him and his father unlock the secrets of leaping back once already.

"But we got hasty," he says, holding up one finger. "My Aunt Lillian got in the way and tried to sabotage our research. So we attempted to leap back before we were actually ready. And, well, we failed. We didn't go back far enough."

Orion can see that I don't believe him. I study my shoes that I'm still holding. "I know this literally sounds like apples and bananas," Orion says, invading my space on all fours. "But you have to believe me. We *need* to figure this out!"

"Why?" I ask, refusing eye contact.

"Because the world needs fixing, Christopher Fritz. And you know that better than anybody." And those words echo around in my bones and in my soul for a long moment. Orion doesn't know about Dad. But he's right. I think about Dad leaving on that Saturday night during Oakley's party. How easily I could have stopped him if I had known what was going to happen. But now there are two unfinished stories from that day.

And then my brain betrays me. I wonder if maybe Orion is telling the truth. After all, he seems to know a lot.

Plot idea: *Boy trades his sanity for a lottery ticket.*

"So why do you remember me, but I don't remember you?" I ask.

"That's my biggest question mark," he says with a finger at his chin. "My father might have some ideas."

"I seriously don't know anything about time travel," I say.

Orion smiles. "Oh, Christopher Fritz. You don't have to." He retrieves the book from his nightstand. *The Little Prince.* "It's not as complicated as you think." He fans through the book. I can see dozens of lines highlighted in green, and pencil writing and arrows assaulting almost every margin. Even in the illustrations. "My father is one of many people who have been trying to answer big questions like this. We think this author was on to something. This story is full of *coded language,* as my father would say." He shakes the book and something falls out of it, clanking against the floor. It's a silver key on a long black string.

"What's the key?"

"It's an unanswered question!" he says. "My father gave this to me and said there are amazing mysteries out there worth solving. I use it as my bookmark." Orion speaks fast. Like, caffeinated hummingbird fast. My brain can't keep up. I wonder if Orion might be the most masterful pretender in the history of kids.

His red clock shows 4:45. Mom is going to start worrying soon.

"Hey, it's nice to meet you and stuff, but I need to go. This sounds like a lot of make-believe."

"I understand that," Orion says. He places his hands on my knees. He sure is a touchy kid. "But I think I can *make you believe.*" The minute changes. "I remember a lot about you from your first move here and all the things we did." His words are an anchor, rooting me to the rug.

"Prove it then." I cross my arms. Orion sits up tall and confident.

"You have a sister named Oakley. She's a second grader and her nickname is Spiral."

"I bet you could hear her singing earlier. She's good at getting attention."

"Your mom is a photographer," he continues. "She used to do baby pictures from home, but now she's going to teach photography at the high school here. She starts tomorrow."

"You could have read that on a school website or some-thing," I retort, pointing to his computer. I uncross my arms. Orion hits me with the same look Oakley has when she's about to play a winning card in Uno. I bite my bottom lip.

"You had plans to go to Seattle this summer. But the trip got canceled because your dad's in prison."

Plot idea: *Boy dares lightning to strike him; gets struck by lightning.*

CHAPTER 5

Heart People, Brain People

SOMEWHERE IN THE WORLD, A TORNADO JUST touched down. All of my feelings get summoned together and tangle themselves up in knots. Orion tries to tell me it's okay. He can see it all on my face, I know he can. A messy meet-up of sadness and embarrassment. My words have all abandoned me again. My understanding of the world just got shot full of holes by a time traveling weirdo with strappy shoes. There's no way this kid could have known about Dad. He must be telling the truth.

And that scares me a little bit. Or a lot.

But in the middle of this mire of feelings, there is something else I can feel. It's a tiny, tiny flame of something good. Just a flicker. But it's burning hot and bright, pulsing through me with something I haven't felt since Dad left on that Saturday night. Its glow fills me up and empties me out.

Plot idea: *Boy empties the well of tears, finds treasure at the bottom.*

"You're such a heart person," Orion says. He's offering a friendly smile. I pat my eyes dry with my navy-blue sleeves. "That's why we need you."

"What?" I ask breathlessly.

"My father says that there are heart people and brain people. Having a heart person like you on our team is important because you see the world differently than we do." He waits for me to finish sniffling, which I sort of appreciate, but I also don't. "We can do this, Christopher Fritz. Your dad needs you."

"What do I have to do?" My voice cracks.

"Leaping back isn't about crazy technology and machines," Orion says, fanning randomly through the pages of *The Little Prince.* "It's about creating a timeline of the things that are *essential.*"

"Like what?"

"Read this." He hands me his book and puts the black string key on himself like a necklace. "It all starts here." The book is light and well-loved. Several of the pages are folded over. I wonder what it might feel like to hold a magic lamp. Just a trinket to one person. An answer to a prayer for another. I've never felt so powerful holding a book before. *Time travel,* I think. *A way to get Dad back.*

The rumbling of a car rolling up to the house shakes the entire world and Orion's eyebrows launch.

"Hide!" he says. He lifts the kiwi-colored skirting of his bed and I scramble underneath, holding his book near to me. The skirting lifts up again and Orion tosses my shoes under. One hits me in the head. "Sorry!" he says. Now I get why Orion told me to carry the shoes.

I can see the reflection of Orion's red clock through the fish tank. I read 4:52 backwards. I really need to get home soon.

"This will be fast, just be quiet," Orion says from above me as though he read my mind. What a strange half hour it has been since I left for my walk.

The front door to the house opens and shuts. Strong steps immediately start up the twelve stairs to Orion's room. I wonder if human breathing can be heard. I also wonder how hard it would be to set the world record for the longest breath-hold ever. I'm not gambling it. I suck in as much air as I can.

A woman's voice greets Orion, and he doesn't say anything back. The glint of Orion's lamplight is bright in her shiny black shoes, and that's all I can see of her. Professional vibe.

"Grab your jacket, kiddo. Dinner with Dad tonight." Her voice is strong, but tired. Orion says okay, then I count all twelve steps again as Orion and I are left alone. He leans over his bed and looks at me upside down, his wispy brown hair grazing the floor.

"Is that your mom?" I ask as quietly as I can.

"No, I don't have a mom," he whispers. "That's my Aunt Lillian. From Arizona." He had mentioned her once before.

"Is she visiting?"

"Nope. She literally got fired and needs a place to stay, so my father agreed to take her in. It's both temporary and terrible." Orion slaps the floor.

"Why am I hiding? Are you in trouble?" Orion scans the room as if he is suspicious of spies.

"My Aunt Lillian is an evil harpy wildebeest who literally hates kids and hates fun and hates the research my father and I are doing."

"Oh." A far cry from what I expected him to say. Having only seen her shoes, I picture fiendishly purple eyes and snakes for hair. A child-eating chimera with a forked tongue and an ax on the end of a slippery, nightmarish tail. I would love to illustrate that.

"She's the one who messed everything up in the first place, so we need to be extra careful around her this time." He pulls me out from under the bed and puts on an electric green winter jacket that says *Untouchable* when he zips it up.

"Wait here in my room," he says softly. "Once we drive away, use the kitchen door to leave. We never lock it. She'll never know you were here" I nod. "Christopher Fritz, she *cannot* know you were here. Tell. Nobody. Not even your mom or sister. People cannot know what my father and I are doing. Please."

I assure him that nobody would believe me even if I did tell. "Do you go to Weston Elementary?" I ask as Orion heads for the stairs.

"No way. I'm homeschooled." He laughs, but I don't really get why.

"Oh."

"You'll like Mr. Tippin," Orion says. "You did last time."

He skips every other stair on his way down. I hear chatter followed by a door closing followed by a car starting and buzzing away down Willoughby Lane.

Being alone in someone else's house makes me feel like I've just rolled in mud before church. I take Orion's book in two hands and, with twelve long steps down, I move as quietly as I can for the kitchen.

When we rushed up to Orion's room, I hadn't noticed how empty the living room was. Virtual grey scale with far more open space than furniture. The carpets are well-kept, the kitchen is impossibly clean, and the faded smell of Windex is on everything. Makes my brain go back to my Oregon house when we were trying to sell. People were coming and going daily, and Mom was a real handful then about keeping everything spotless and orderly. If this house were edible, Orion's bedroom would be a heap of rainbow sprinkles capping off this room's cone of freezer-burnt vanilla. Both are a little much for me in different ways.

I reach the kitchen door that leads into the back yard, but my eyes catch the corner of a square photo resting next to a tall stack of envelopes. There are two people in the picture. One is Orion, wearing the same shiny golden scarf as today, and he's laughing a real big laugh. The other must be his dad, a slender and smart looking man with thin grey glasses and no hair. He's holding Orion close and in his eyes I can see the same proud look that my dad used to give me. My heart pumps hard and my fingers curl into fists.

Plot idea: *Boy breaks into palace, burns the whole place down.*

CHAPTER 6

Cosmic Transmission

MOM SAYS THAT I OVERTHINK THINGS
when I say that God doesn't have time to hear
prayers. I try to tell her that if even one percent of Earth's
people are praying at the same time, that's more than seventy-million things to listen to at once. And I struggled
back in Oregon when just Flint and Calvin would talk at
the same time. Somewhere in the world, those two are
probably badgering each other right now. Makes my guts
get all twisted up to think about how much I miss them.

And Dad, too. God may not have time for my words,
but Dad is just one person. I like to think that he can feel
my energy and words coming to him like a cosmic transmission every night. I tuck my thumbs into my fists and
transmit with all I've got while I walk.

*I've got it, Dad. I'm going to fix everything. There's a
neighbor kid here on Willoughby Lane who knows how to go*

back in time. I didn't believe at first, but he knows everything about me. And about you. He's kind of weird, but in a nice way. And if he can get things back to normal, I'll do whatever he needs. I'm coming, Dad. Hang tight. Transmit back.

"That was a long walk, Critter." Mom is at the stove adding salt to a pot of noodles.

"Well look, he has a book," Oakley adds from the dining room table. She's pointing at *The Little Prince*. I'm grateful for her saying that. I don't really feel like explaining what has taken place this afternoon. That, and Orion told me not to.

It makes my brain go backwards to see all of our furniture in new places. I'm trying to hang onto the picture in my head of how things used to look back in Oregon. In this house, there is barely enough space for us to fit all four chairs around the table. Makes me wonder why we even have all four out.

"I'll set up," I say. And I hunt around for the new home of the forks and plates.

Over dinner, Mom explains what tomorrow is going to be like. The walk, the teachers, the afternoon plan. It'll be the first day of school here for all of us. Oakley and I will be walking a few blocks to our new school. Weston Elementary is two stories bigger and probably five decades younger than my old school. We drove by it as soon as we arrived and, truthfully, I am excited to see the inside. Any place where I am expected to read and not talk is a fine place in my life.

Mom will be driving clear across town to Cortland High School. Home of the Cougars and the only high school in this miniature mistake of a town. Mom isn't a real teacher, but they hired her on as an emergency photography teacher because the real one up and quit mid-year. I only half listen to the table talk. My brain is stuck thinking about my time traveling neighbor and the book he wants me to read. If Orion knows how to get Dad back, then garlic pasta and school small talk isn't high on my priority list.

"Share one thing you're excited about for tomorrow," Mom says.

Oakley pounds the table with one fist and accidentally sends her fork flying past her shoulder. I never fell into the bottomless pit of school-hatred like Oakley has. She could probably set a world record for most whining about school ever by a second grader. She's too wiry and busy to sit and focus, which is probably why the tears are starting to come down and she's begging Mom to not make her go.

"What if the teachers are mean?"

"Then you'll learn about how to be agreeable," Mom says as she sneaks a picture of Oakley with her head on the table.

"What if the kids don't like me?" She's turned her help-less voice up to the max setting.

"Spiral, I'm sure there will be kids there who are just as nice as Maddie and Caroline," Mom says, referring to

Oakley's band of trouble-making, Disney-loving besties back home.

"I know what I'm excited for," I say without looking up. "I won't have to listen to your pathetic whining all day." Oakley inhales sharply. My words came out with more heat than I intended.

"Excuse me, Chris," Mom says, taking control. "Care to try that again?"

I drop the fork and lean back in my chair. "I'm sorry. I didn't mean—"

"Ever since Dad left you've been such a jerk!" Oakley slams her chair into the table and the door behind her to her bedroom. Our dinner and the table talk have both been canceled. Just like the Seattle trip. Just like my picture book author career.

Plot idea: *Boy pulls rabbit out of a hat, accidentally rips the ears off.*

I fold my arms and rest my head on them. I wonder if I can trace my entire shoelace with my finger before Mom rips into me. I don't even get halfway. The next three minutes are a been-there-done-that lecture about finding strength in a difficult situation, grit, and the importance of using my words correctly. "Your dad wouldn't want to hear you talk like that," Mom says at one point. I imagine how good it would feel to set a world record for digging the biggest hole ever and pushing all of Cortland into it, including Mom. I'm given my orders: apologize to Oakley, then unpack my room.

"Okay," I say, knowing that I'm not going to do either.

If Orion really can prevent this train wreck of a move, unpacking is a total waste of my time. I go to my room. I open Orion's book. This is what matters most right now.

CHAPTER 7

The Nons

"HELLO, YOUNG MAN," MR. TIPPIN SAYS AS he shakes my hand. "Welcome to Weston Elementary." The green of his long tie reminds me of both Mountain Dew and of Orion's winter coat. *Untouchable.* I hang up my backpack in the hallway and Mr. Tippin leads me inside a very empty, very calm classroom. More vanilla. All the other kids were playing outside when I arrived. But there is one boy here with spiky red hair that is far too red to be natural. He has one arm in a sling. Mr. Tippin takes me to the cluster of desks where the boy is sitting and he taps a nameplate that has my full name in delightfully curly cursive, something I never learned how to use.

I take my seat. I love the feeling of having a spot that's mine.

"Mr. Fritz," he says, "What do you like to be called?"

"Chris, I guess."

He nods. He then gestures to the boy sitting next to me. "Chris, I'd like you to meet Mr. Rhett Robbins." Rhett waves at me with his non-injured hand. "Rhett is our leader of the week, and he also helps manage the Junior Surge Swim Team."

Rhett smiles real proud at that.

"Rhett here is going to help you out with anything you need. Please feel free to ask."

I wonder if Rhett has to babysit me because he is the leader of the week, or if he is leader of the week because he volunteered to do it. Or maybe he can't play outside because of his injury.

Mr. Tippin asks for my permission to introduce me to the class when they arrive. I'm surprised to be asked for permission for something by a teacher. My Oregon teachers would have never done that. Their class, their castle.

A morning bell rings and Mr. Tippin leaves to fetch the rest of the class. On the way out, he asks Rhett to show me the materials already stashed away in my desk. Mr. Tippin has a crisp enunciation when he talks. It's the opposite of Orion, whose hasty words turned to applesauce as soon as they reached his teeth yesterday. If Mr. Tippin weren't a teacher, he'd probably be a radio host or an emcee or something. He's well-practiced.

The classroom isn't wall-to-wall charts and graphs like my old one. We had so many handwritten posters and signs that you couldn't ever find even three inches of wall space. The whiteboard has an agenda and the date written on the left side. And other than a room-long number line and word wall, this is the most blank classroom I've ever been in. It's a void. Reminds me a lot of Orion's living room. And then I wonder if ignoring interior design is just a Cortland thing.

Rhett offers me a handshake and repeats his name. "Rhett Robbins. And no restaurant jokes, please." I take his handshake and he rolls his eyes when I give a long *yuuum.* "It's nice to meet you, dude."

He's unfairly skinny, and his face has a nice round shape.

"What happened to your arm?" I ask.

"I got into a little fight," he says matter-of-factly, like he's telling me what day of the week it is.

"Oh, wow." That reminds me of the tackle yesterday. I thought Orion was going to punch my face off. But now I know he was just happy to see me again. "I'm sorry. About the fight." I wonder if I also met Rhett the first time I moved here. And then a question blitzes through me and out of my mouth before my brain even realizes it. "Rhett, do you remember me?"

He tilts his chin in confusion. *That was stupid.*

"We just met, dude."

"Right, sorry. You just look familiar," I lie. He shrugs. Somewhere in the world, the tooth fairy just forgot to visit.

The desks in the classroom begin to fill. I study each face as kids find their spots and, as if in return, each one looks me over. A girl with short blond hair fills the open desk at our cluster.

"Hi, I'm Ava," she says as she offers to shake my hand. It's my third handshake of the day, and I'm starting to detect an unfamiliar professionalism here. I expected noise and motion to seize the morning like I'm used to, but students find their desks and immediately pull out books. Silent reading. Mr. Tippin hasn't even said a word.

I don't have a book with me. *The Little Prince* is still at my house, and I finished that last night anyway. What an odd story it was, too. I sit silently, trying and failing to not feel awkward about not having something to read. I see other kids glance sneakily in my direction. Second takes. A lot of kids are simply pretending to read. I've done that enough to know what it looks like. Mr. Tippin rings a small chime on the whiteboard and, as easily as flicking on a light switch, all the books get tucked away and the room is silent. Orion was right. I do like Mr. Tippin already.

"Ladies and gentlemen," Mr. Tippin says, "we have a new member of our learning community. I'd like you to meet Chris Fritz." Other kids take aim at me with smiles and waves. "In celebrating Chris's being here, our morning dialogue will be about places. Where are you from, and where would you like to go? Be thoughtful and be listeners." He snaps his fingers and each group of kids open into conversations about dream vacations and places to visit.

Rhett says that he was born here in Cortland and never wants to leave. Ava wants to visit Holland because she wants to live in some place called Amsterdam, which sounds delightfully like a word she shouldn't say at school.

It's my turn to talk. Rhett and Ava are waiting for me to say something. The words in my brain are tangling up. "Uh, I'm from Oregon." They nod, as if asking me to keep going. "And now I live here." *Again, stupid.*

"Do you live near the school?" Ava asks.

"Kind of. I live over on Willoughby Lane." Ava's eyes widen and she sits up.

"Does Orion McBride still live there?"

"Ava, stop," Rhett interrupts with a groan. "The nons?" He raises his eyebrows to her.

"What are the nons?" I ask. Mr. Tippin hears my question and strikes his chime once again.

"Fifth graders, I'd like to teach Chris about our nons, and attending to fundamentals is always a worthwhile review." I shrug at Ava. "We have three nons in this classroom that must always be observed. What is the first non?"

"No talking about people who aren't in the room," the entire class answers in slow litany. That must be why Rhett stopped Ava.

"Non number two?"

"No put-downs of ourselves, each other, or the material."

"Non number three?"

"Don't put yourself ahead of the learning community."

Plot idea: *Boy gets drafted into the army, loves every second.*

"Fifth graders, please open your math books. Page ninety."

CHAPTER 8

Climbing

THE SCHOOL DAY WENT AS QUICKLY AS IT came. Class with Mr. Tippin is fast-paced and efficient. "Concision and precision, fifth graders," he said during both math and writing.

Honestly, it's hard to focus on persuasive writing and decimals when all I want to do is find Orion. Getting comfy at Weston Elementary is pointless. After all, if Orion and I leap back in time and stop Dad, I'll never arrive in Cortland to begin with. When Rhett was trying to get me to join the swim team during lunch, I wanted to tell him that I wouldn't be staying long. *I've got other places and times to be,* I imagined myself saying.

I check the gym to make sure Oakley made it to the after-school group. I try to wave at her, but she and a girl with a dusty black ponytail are in full play mode. Back in Oregon, you were more likely to spot a bald eagle perched on a cross than a happy Oakley after a day of school, so I decide to let her be. The plan is for her to stay with the afterschool group until Mom can pick her up. But fourth and fifth graders are too old for the afterschool program. That's why I'm headed to the Cortland Community Library. Mom says she isn't ready to give me a key to the house because she's thinks I'd eat all the food. "Spiral and I need to eat, too," she had teased when we discussed after-school plans.

Three blocks to Willoughby Lane, then two more blocks to the library. I'm thankful that the sun has shooed away the clouds. My Mariners hoodie is actually enough warmth today. I skip-step as I near Willoughby Lane because in the yard next to mine, I can see the exact golden scarf that I was hoping I'd see. Orion is dribbling a basketball in the empty driveway. His cocoa-colored hair is a tangled, unbrushed mess. Mom's stuffing would come out if I left the house like that without a hat.

He sees me when I am two houses away. I stop and brace myself in case he is going to charge at me again. But he waves and keeps dribbling his ball, sometimes using both hands to keep control. "Hi, Christopher Fritz." His voice is like a flute against the bass drum beat of his ball. "Ready to go?"

"I can't come in today, I have to—"

"Go to the library. I know." He catches his ball and grabs a backpack off his doorstep. It's covered in planets, stars, and a silver rocket swirling through space. "We've done this before, remember?"

Right.

Plot idea: *Boy with amnesia marvels as he reads about his own misadventures.*

The walk to the library isn't filled with the buzz and questions and answers I had been daydreaming about at school. Instead, I walk to the thump of Orion's basketball, which scurries into the street twice before we even reach the end of Willoughby Lane. He's not the most coordinated boy in town, that's for sure.

"Did you start *The Little Prince?*" he asks.

"I read it all last night. It was pretty short."

"So? What did you think?"

"I don't really get it. And I don't get how leaping through time has anything to do with it. It was just a story." Orion chuckles, which makes me feel a tiny bit insulted. I want him to explain what he means, but I don't even know what questions to ask. I change the subject instead.

"What's it like to be homeschooled?"

"It's literally the best ever. My father teaches me all the school stuff in the morning, and in the afternoon it's research time." Orion carries his ball after losing it for a third time. "He's out conducting studies on temporal flux right now." He's trying to make that sound important, but I don't need convincing. "He's a very solitary man, Christopher Fritz. So, I'll be doing all the communicating between us."

We cross Tenth Street, and the library comes into view with its satisfying circular brickwork. The tree near the entrance would make a perfect shaded reading spot in the summertime. It's a nice daydream, but then I remember I probably won't be here to enjoy that. It's a worthy sacrifice. Orion stuffs his ball into his backpack and his hands into the pockets of his purple shorts as we reach the fork. Left into the children's library. Right into the adult library. Orion leads me left. The librarian with marshmallow-white hair is at the circulation desk. "Hi, Stormy," Orion says.

"Hey hey, Booker!" she answers.

"Templeton!" Orion spits out with surprising volume.

"What?" I ask.

"You're the newcomer I met yesterday," the librarian says. "I'm Stormy. And I see you've already met Booker," she says with a wave to Orion.

"Templeton!" Orion chirps again. His eyes are locked on her, but he's grinning that freckly grin. Orion has a way of switching between well-spoken-sciency mode and feisty-playful-puppy mode on a whim. Whatever is going on here has brought out his inner pup.

"Is this a game?" I ask.

Orion covers his heart like I've just shot him point blank. "My favorite book is *not* a game," he says.

Stormy laughs. I ask him what the book is, but he tells me to *stay put* and scurries off to the shelves. Stormy holds her hands up for two high fives that I accept gladly. We trade introductions and she confirms that I'm staying here until my mom can pick me up.

"Your mom said you might want to be an author some-day?" she asks.

"I used to want to," I say. "I don't really know." My brain goes backwards to Oregon. To that Saturday. To Oakley's party. Somewhere in the world, a pen dries out. Stormy gestures to the hundreds of books in the library and says that if I ever get published, she'd buy a copy of my book and make a Local Authors section right here. That brings me back to the present real fast.

Plot idea: *Boy builds a castle with the remnants of his shattered home.*

The library's colors and design remind me of Orion's coloring book bedroom. There's even a tree loft and, if it weren't for the mother and child already reading in it, I might have already climbed up. There are low cubbies full of picture books just before dozens of shelves where Orion is scanning the chapter books.

Picture books are a guilty pleasure of mine. The boxes in my room hide dozens of my creations. Volumes upon volumes of printer paper, staples, and colored pencil scratchings. My own ideas, tales, and musings. I used to read them to Oakley, but she hasn't asked in quite a while. And I don't really want to see them anyway.

"Watch this," Stormy says to me. "Booker!"

"Templeton!" Orion sings from somewhere among the books.

"I don't get it," I say.

"It's our little joke from a book called *Onwards and Backwards.* A littler version of Orion read it and one hundred percent flipped out about how much he enjoyed it.

The names are a running joke between characters. He'd say it over and over until all of us here finally started calling him—" she cups her mouth with her hands and barks, "Booker!"

"Templeton!" Orion answers as he returns with the book Stormy mentioned. *Onwards and Backwards.* "You'll love this," he says as he tosses it to Stormy. "Check it out with my name, please."

Stormy's fingernails work the keys and she scans the book before handing it to me. Orion tells Stormy that *we have business to attend to* and she wishes us a swell day. That's when I notice a new Book of the Day: *The Rift of Sound and Light.*

"This cover is so pretty," I say picking it up.

"Spoken like a true heart boy," Orion says teasingly. I try to slap him with the book, but he spins out of the way. He grabs at my backpack and I am busy shaking him off when I notice someone from the other side of the library watching this play moment unfold. It's the girl from class. It's Ava. Orion notices me wave in her direction. He shoves me toward the sliding door with both hands. "Let's go. We have a mission."

I follow Orion out and around to the backside of the library. I tell him that I'm supposed to stay here, but he assures me that we aren't going anywhere. "I want to show you something," he says. He guides me to an air conditioning unit that is just out of sight from the parking lot. He climbs on top of it and jumps for a low, thin tree branch to pull himself up. From there, he jumps. In about two seconds flat, Orion is standing on a thin ledge that loops around the entire midsection of the library. He's probably ten feet off the ground.

"So when do we do the time travel stuff?" I ask.

"Hush up and climb," he answers.

And so I do. The safety alarm that Mom lectured into my brain's software is going off. In fact, it's the second day in a row that I've found myself following Orion into a weird situation. Mom sometimes says: *Fool me once, shame on you; fool me twice, shame on me.* I don't think Orion is trying to fool me, but I nearly die of a heart attack when the tree branch creaks under my feet.

We're halfway between the ground and the roof. If this ledge were on the ground, it'd be nothing to walk on. Like the perimeter of a playground, or the cement blocks that stop cars in parking spaces. But this feels like a bad kind of different and I can hear God telling me to turn around. I ask Orion how he knows about this.

"Homeschoolers have a lot of time to explore." He laughs.

I'm feeling just a little bit jealous of Orion's *self-fastening* shoes and, in them, his tiny feet. I scoot forward inch by inch by inch. After what feels like five days of peril, Orion impatiently points up to a gap in the design of the brick near the roof.

"Easy part," he says as he hops, grabs, and pulls himself up to the roof with two climbs. Orion's done this before. This entire climb is totally out of the way of the parking lot and side street. The fear of my mom watching me grabs hold of my soul and I double take. But the coast is clear, and I ignore Orion's outstretched hand as I make my way up.

"Welcome to my favorite place," Orion says as we stand on the top of the Cortland Community Library.

"This is awesome," I say. From this two-story rooftop, it's easy to look out over most of our one-story town. I can see Willoughby Lane and, just beyond it, I have a full view of Weston Elementary School. The mountains that dwarf Cortland glow brilliantly in the evening sun. Radiant peaks and valleys of gold and blue.

From up here I should easily be able to see Mom's car coming, though I'm not really sure how we're going to get down when that time comes. I can already hear the scolding I'd get if she caught me up here. She never gives it a rest about safety stuff. I push that thought away and join Orion who is dangling his legs over the edge of the roof.

"So, Christopher Fritz. Let's talk about the leaping." He opens up his galactic backpack and pulls out the basketball. "My father is the brains behind literally all of it. I sort of understand it, but it's complicated." He's faking an English accent.

"Well yesterday I didn't even think it could happen at all."

"My father says that to weave through time, we have to know what's *essential*." He holds up the ball. "See how all these lines on the ball start at the bottom and split off in different directions? Those are like timelines. And we're here." He points to the middle of one of the black lines. "We need to be over here," and he points to the next line over. "But we can't just jump line-to-line. We have to go back to the bottom where all the lines split apart." His speedy words are turning to applesauce again.

"How?"

"By creating a sequence of the *essential* moments." He keeps using that word. "And the essential stuff, Christopher Fritz, is invisible." That last word comes out in a whisper.

He's got that frosty look in his eyes again. I can see those wild horses making noise in his head. A low rumble.

"We have to find something invisible? That's impossible," I say. Orion pulls something else out of his backpack. A boxy white and blue Polaroid camera. My cousins back in Oregon had one just like it, except in neon pink. *AM/OM* is written in black marker near the lens.

Now I know where all of the square pictures on Orion's bulletin board came from.

He holds the camera out in front of us and I smile instinctively. He clicks. Almost instantly, Orion is holding a little square of us. We're squinting in the light of the setting sun and Orion's head is almost totally sideways, tilted toward me. His unkempt hair and sunny golden scarf frame his face perfectly. I wonder out loud if his camera can capture the invisible subjects we need.

"I sure hope so." He laughs and takes out a note card from the pocket of his grape-juice shorts. It has something written in thick, black marker lines written on the lined side. It says *Mission: Watch a sunset.* He paperclips the picture to the note card.

"That's it?" I glance out at the orange and purple splashes in the western sky. "That was the mission?"

"That's just step one. My father will give us a new mission when he's ready." Orion unsuccessfully tries to spin his ball on one finger before loading it up in his backpack with his camera. He swings the bag over his shoulder. The note card and picture rest between us and I sneak another look. This all makes me wonder how hard this whole *leaping* thing is actually going to be.

Plot idea: *Boy wins chess tournament without ever moving a single piece.*

"Hey, there's something I was thinking about today," I say after a minute of quiet.

"Go on."

"You said the world needs fixing," I'm trying to mask my hesitation as Orion rests his chin on a closed fist. "What are you trying to fix?"

Orion takes a deep breath in and holds it for at least a month before letting it go. "I want to stop my aunt from moving in with us. Things have changed since she arrived. It's not been good."

"She can't really be that bad, can she?"

Orion doesn't answer. He holds his basketball with both hands and turns his body away from me. "It's just, umm," he starts. But he doesn't get the rest out.

I can feel the universe roll its eyes at me. There I go again. Ruining a moment with careless words. I guess it's really none of my business why Orion wants to go back in time. I should have realized that. But I thought it seemed fair because of what he knows about me. Orion is now completely motionless, arms around his legs.

A familiar smell floats through the air and takes me by surprise. It swings my stomach into overdrive. It's the smell of popcorn. Buttery, gooey popcorn. Over on Main Street I can see what looks to be the movie theater here in Cortland. The only one in town. I had asked to go yesterday—anything to avoid unpacking—but Mom said they only show evening movies. With the sun sitting low on the edge of my world, they're probably just now opening for the night.

Orion mumbles something into his legs.

"What?" I ask, looking for his buried face.

Orion launches to his feet and screams to all of Cortland, "I said I hate that smell!"

I recoil. I can see the veins in his arms. The wild horses behind his eyes are rushing now. Unleashed. He claps his basketball with a mighty *thwack* and drop-kicks it off the roof, clear into the atmosphere with a scream.

"What the heck, Orion?" I ask, but it doesn't come out like a question. I watch the ball soar behind a line of trees and listen for its impact. When I look back at Orion, he's on his knees. Eyes down. Two hands on his head like he's about to rip out hair by the fistful. Looks like a total malfunction.

It puts Oakley's unexpected flare-ups to shame. "Orion, are you okay?"

Plot idea: *Boy calls 911 to ask for emergency phone number.*

The next moment is the longest one I've had since moving to Cortland. I'm motionless. Waiting for Orion to do something. Or say something. But he doesn't. I know I have quite the track record of making matters worse when I open my mouth, but I risk it. "Orion?" I ask. "What's wrong?"

His head stays down. He inhales really big and lets out all of the air slowly. He does it twice.

"I'm sorry, Christopher Fritz." Normal color is returning to his face.

I ask him if he wants me to leave, but he shakes his head no. He drops his feet over the side of the building again. "Do you need anything?" I ask. And this time he shakes his head yes. He pats for me to join him on the edge.

"We just need to stay focused on the missions," he says. Low voice. "The world needs fixing. And we don't have forever."

"Right. The world needs fixing," I repeat. He squints like he's looking for something far away. I wonder what he must be going through. About how bad his aunt must be to cause that kind of meltdown. And then I remember what I'm trying to fix. "Hey, Orion?" I ask. He looks at me. "Can you really help me get my dad back? Like, for real?"

Orion's flat stare turns into a slight grin. "Oh, Christopher Fritz," he says, eyes still on the horizon. "I can't wait for you to see how it works again. It's my most marvelous invention." He puts one arm around my shoulder.

There's that flame inside me again. My way back home. My solution. The answer that Dad needs. I never would have guessed that it would be a cartoony ten-year-old to show me the way. But here I am. And if Orion needs me to stay focused, there's nothing in the world that's going to distract me from the missions. Not when my summer with Dad might actually be back on. I can't help but smile at that.

"I have one more question for you," I say. "It's really important."

"Okay."

"Do you always wear shorts in January?" And he rolls his eyes and laughs. I put my arm around his shoulder, mirroring him. We enjoy the last few minutes of the sun slipping away from an orange Cortland sky. The stars will begin peeping through any minute now.

I've never wondered about connecting stars like dots on paper, but this seems like the perfect place to lie back and do it. It's a bit of a shame that I won't be here to do something like that once it's warmer. Not if we're successful with the missions.

"I've missed you," Orion says.

We only just met yesterday. Or, met *again*, I guess. But I feel so connected to Orion. I hope that when we leap back this time, I can remember him, too.

CHAPTER 9

Blues and Greens

MOM HASN'T FIGURED OUT THE NEW RADIO
stations here yet, so we ride to the tune of
scratchy breaks and bouncing gravel. My brain is stuck
thinking about Orion. It puzzles me how he can be a chirpy
puppy-kid screeching "Templeton!" one minute, and ready
to punt his ball across the country the next. We'll meet
again tomorrow, but not on Thursday because of Orion's
hockey practice. Makes me wonder how a boy who needs
two hands to dribble a basketball would do on ice skates,
but maybe that's the point.

We pick up tacos on the way home because Mom says
she is too tired to cook. Oakley snickers from the back
seat when Mom asks for no lettuce on mine. "Picky, picky,
picky," she sings. I want to fire back, but I remember what
happened last night and just count streetlights instead.
I've never seen Mom look this tired at 5:30. I want to have

sympathy for her but moving here to Cortland was her master plan to begin with, so I can't feel bad for that.

There are twenty-nine streetlights between Taco Bell and Willoughby Lane.

There's a freshly washed black sports car in Orion's driveway. Arizona plates. This is the first time I've seen a car parked at his house. I'm worried about Orion's drop-kick tantrum from earlier. Something about his aunt really got under his skin. *Untouchable* might be rounding up.

Plot idea: *Monochromatic dragon versus the boy who wields the colors.* I bet Oakley would enjoy that one.

After we eat, Mom tells us to fix up our hair so we can take new first-day-of-school pictures. Pictures were part of the morning plan, but Mom was worried about being late for her first day. She lines us up by the front door and brings out the good camera. The one with a thick black neck strap and removable lens. She tells me to take off my Mariners hoodie because I look like I slob. She doesn't like it when I say that slobbery is my most natural state.

Oakley holds up two fingers and I hold up five.

"Critter, smile," Mom says as several flashes blind us in the living room. I earn a private frown after she checks the display to see how they turned out. "Here, let's take some from a different angle. The lighting is poor that way."

"No thanks, I'm done," I say.

"What?" Mom sounds surprised.

"No more pictures, please. I'm tired." I head for my supply closet of a bedroom. I can feel Oakley and Mom looking at each other as I leave.

I grab *Onwards and Backwards* from my backpack and study its quirky cover. There's a silver medal on the cover that I've never seen before. The award has a subtle bumpy texture that feels nice under my thumb.

Twenty minutes into the story, Orion's "*Booker! Templeton!*" routine makes a whole lot more sense. Makes me smile to imagine a younger Orion devouring this book and parading it about at the library for all the employees. *He sure is an oddball,* I think. *Dad would love him.* But my reading is interrupted by Oakley pushing open my door with her foot.

She's holding a pencil pox in one hand and Stardust's mangled ear in the other. I wonder what the world would look like if Stardust left a royal blue trail wherever she was dragged. The lines would be visible from space.

"Want to make a book?" she asks, holding out her tools

I always loved making books with Oakley back in Oregon. She's a far better illustrator than I am, and I know more words, so we're pretty much a dream team at this sort of thing. But ever since Dad left on that Saturday night, I've sworn off making books.

"No," I answer. Her lip curls up and I return to the story in my hands.

"I was just thinking that—"

"I said no." And she puts her supplies on top of a nearby box stack and pouts her way out. Somewhere in the world, a firefly dies. I feel a tiny bit bad about turning her down, but I know that it's a temporary thing. Once Orion and I capture what is *essential*, Oakley and I can go back to a life we never moved away from in the first place. We'll make trilogy after trilogy at a minimum.

A few pages later, I find myself laughing at the story's use of dry humor. But then Mom appears in my doorway, light reflecting in her misty eyes. She's covering her phone's receiver with one hand. "Critter, the phone's for you." She holds it out, smile quivering along with her voice.

"Who is it?" I ask.

"It's your dad."

And with those three words my soul explodes. The whole world explodes and melts and reforms itself. I want to break something. I want to yell until my voice is gone. I want to hear his voice. My hands cover my ears and I choke back my own tears. I didn't know he would be allowed to use a phone. I can hear my own heartbeat. So, so loud.

I miss him. I miss him so much. But I don't want to talk to Dad in prison. I want to talk to Dad in Oregon. I want to talk to him in the kitchen while we make chocolate chip pancakes for Oakley and Mom sleeping in on the weekend. I want to talk to him about how he knows all the random crap on *Jeopardy* that he has no business knowing. I want to talk to him at the Mariners game about what a choke artist the third baseman is and how ballpark food is overpriced. But not like this.

No, I think. Orion will get me home. Orion will make this whole nightmare end. And I'll wake up in Seattle in the summertime. Navy-blue sky, shining green sea. At the game, just Dad and me.

"No," I say. "I don't want to talk." My eyes are shut and I've covered my ears, but in the air between us I can still feel the fracturing of something inside Mom. I peek. Mom and I share the longest, most person-crushing eye contact mankind has ever known. I've never seen her give me this look before. It's a place where shock and sorrow and disappointment join together.

"Shaun, your son isn't feeling great tonight. Maybe next time." Her gaze impales me. And it hurts.

Plot idea: *Boy needs to stay warm, commits arson.*

My page in *Onwards and Backwards* is all soggy and crumpled up. I fling the book away, hoping it will explode into letters and dust and I wonder for the first time if anybody has ever drowned in their own tears.

CHAPTER 10

The Cardinal

I DON'T GET TO GO OUT FOR MORNING RECESS ON my second day. At first I thought I had done something wrong, like violate one of the classroom nons or something. But Rhett tells me that everyone in the class has to do private conferences with Mr. Tippin every now and then. He does two every day. Since I'm the new kid in class, I get bumped to the top of the list. Stellar.

Mr. Tippin sits across from me and thumbs through a blue paper folder with my name on the tab, last then first. It's probably information from my old school. Gives me goosebumps all down my legs to think about what those papers say about me. I know what I'd put down if it was me making that folder: *Chris Fritz. Good at reading. Okay at writing. Sucks at pretty much everything else.*

"How was your first day? Are you feeling okay about everything?" Mr. Tippin closes the folder and folds his hands.

"Yeah, it's okay."

"Have you connected with anybody yet?"

That makes my brain leap straight to Orion. I remember the smell of popcorn from the roof of the Cortland Community Library and I feel warm all over. That flame. But I doubt Mr. Tippin knows Orion. "Rhett's nice," I answer.

"He is indeed," Mr. Tippin says. "Your records show that you are quite the reader." I nod. "What have you read lately?"

"Well I read a book called *Onwards and Backwards* yesterday. And *The Little Prince* on Monday."

"Goodness. Two books in two days?" He uses his tie to wipe away some fingerprints on his glasses. "That's an extraordinary amount of time with novels." He leans in. "Is everything okay at home?"

"Yeah, things are fine," I lie.

"Chris, we know you've been through a lot in the last six months."

My jaw tightens up and I wonder how much trouble I would get for strangling a teacher with his own tie. I don't care what's in that blue folder. Mr. Tippin has no idea what last fall was like. Being trapped in a flaming tornado would be less painful than moving to Willoughby Lane.

"Yeah. It's been pretty sucky," I admit.

"If you ever want to talk or take a break, please ask. We're all here for you, Chris."

I thank him and my hands retreat into the pocket of my Mariners hoodie. Mr. Tippin tells me that on Wednesdays and Fridays we do something called WIN Groups. It stands for *What I Need*. All three fifth grade classes get shuffled up and work on projects that best fit their abilities. For this week, I'll be staying here with Mr. Tippin so the teachers can *calibrate my data*.

Plot idea: *Boy gets poked full of holes by data-driven cyborgs.*

After a total struggle of division practice, it's time for lunch. Rhett stops me on the staircase. "I'm going to find you in the cafeteria. I want to talk to you."

Again, goosebumps. He leaps down the staircase to catch up to a group of boys waiting, but a teacher makes him go all the way back up and use every step. His friends snicker and Rhett has that smile like he's being polite, but he's really just putting on a show for his buddies. Somewhere in the world, Flint and Calvin are doing the exact same thing. He gives a thumbs up from his sling.

I plop down across from Ava with a tray of rectangle pizza and diced peaches swimming in their own juice. Rhett is talking to some other boys at another table, but he waves and gives me the *just one sec* sign. I've already eaten half of my pizza before Ava has taken a single bite. "What were you doing with Orion?" she asks.

She's talking about yesterday at the library. Orion's voice echoes in my brain.

Tell. Nobody.

"He was just showing me around." Rhett tosses his lunch box next to Ava and some cookies and a spoon bounce out. The tiny pepperonis I have are almost the same color as Rhett's cardinal red hair. I hold one up and squint in comparison. He says that my preference for ranch dressing on pizza is *highly offensive,* so I lick it off to be as repulsive as possible.

Ava's unimpressed, but Rhett loves it. Ava mutters something soft about boys as she shakes her head.

"Dude, hear me out," Rhett says. I have a prediction on what he's going to say. "I used to be part of a relay group. Junior Surge Swim Team." Prediction confirmed. "But I can't swim with a broken arm. So now I'm stuck being a manager assistant, and it's crap."

"I'm sorry," I say with a mouthful of doughy crust. It comes out lispy.

"We need one more swimmer or the relay team can't swim."

"And you want me to join?"

"Yes! Dude, it doesn't even matter if you're good."

Ava snorts at that.

"Sorry. I mean, the junior team doesn't even compete. Competition starts in middle school. The junior teams do a few invitationals around the state. No medals. No records. Just swimming and meeting people."

I wonder what Dad would think of me— his indoorsy author child— joining a swim team. I also wonder why the idea of Rhett seeing me in a swimsuit makes me want to throw up all over him.

Plot idea: *Boy turned into a fish by the curse of the cardinal*

It's been a long time since I've swam, but I know how to do it. Dad would take me and Oakley over to Whistler Beach, our favorite coastal getaway. We'd boogie board for hours at a time and eat the world's saltiest French fries on the boardwalk. Dad said that if you swim hard enough, you won't freeze to death in the frigid waters. We learned how to swim real fast that way.

Dad forgot to put sunscreen on our backs the last time we went to Whistler Beach and Oakley and I had to lie down on our bellies during the car trip home because we hurt so bad. There was a lot of crying and a lot of laughing that day. And a lot of really great pictures Mom took when we got home. One of them is hanging in our living room now. But there are no pictures of Dad hanging up. I think I'm the only one who's noticed that.

"I don't know, Rhett. My after-school time is really busy and—"

"We practice before school. At CMS." Rhett is relentless. I can tell he's recruited kids before. "You live on Willoughby Lane, right? We'll pick you up on the way to practice and then take you to school."

I look to Ava, to Rhett, then to my half-eaten lunch.

"Dude. Just give it a try."

There is approximately zero percent of me that wants to give up my mornings to go splash around in some dirty pool, even if Rhett would be there. But there is approximately one hundred percent of me that wants to spend as little time as possible at my bombsite of a house.

CHAPTER 11

Roses

STORMY WAVES AT US WHEN WE ENTER THE library, and she does the same call and response game with Orion. The Wyoming wind is blistering today. Makes me regret only wearing my Mariners hoodie for a jacket, but if Orion can tough through it with those yellow shorts, I'll adapt.

I deposit *Onwards and Backwards* into the book bin and pick up the new Book of the Day: *Quintuplet*.

"So is that your game?" Stormy asks as Orion checks it out for me. "Come in here and just take my Book of the Day every day?" She smiles as she hands it to me. "I might have to call you *Daily* so I can remember what you're all about."

"I still have to read the one from yesterday," I say. "And now this one. This one looks awesome."

"Good thing the weekend's almost here," Stormy says with a wink. Orion tugs at my backpack straps.

"Come on. I wanna show you something," he says as he pulls.

"Have a swell day, boys. Bye, Booker," Stormy says from her desk.

Orion spins around and holds up one demanding finger at her. "Templeton," splitting apart each syllable.

Stormy laughs and waves us along. She's really good at bringing that out of him.

Orion leads me through periodicals and past the adult section circulation desk to a cavernous space with a Local History sign. The walls inside are lined with dozens of maps. Colorful maps, state maps, and some maps with curvy lines and a dozen different shades of green.

In the middle of the local history room is a glass-encased display big enough for an entire class of kids to fit around. At first it looks like it's full of Legos, but they are actually tiny figurines of cars and itty-bitty buildings. They're scattered along a quartz-colored street line that was probably made with a single paintbrush stroke. "Is this our town?" I ask.

"Yep. It's old Cortland."

I recognize some of the buildings along the tiny Main Street. The movie theater is super recognizable. The very library we are standing in sits in the corner of the display. "This is literally how the town looked when my father was a kid." The town has grown. I don't see Weston Elementary and, since the library touches the edge of the case, there is no Willoughby Lane either.

"This feels like time travel," I say. Orion gives me a knowing smile and rolls his eyes. I toss my book on the glass.

"Our next mission is a tricky one, Christopher Fritz." He adopts his English accent again. "We have to find a flower. But not just any flower." He pulls a note card from his pocket and puts it in my face. It reads: *Find something worth keeping.* "We need to find a rose."

"A rose? In January?" I remember reading about a rose in *The Little Prince*. I'm struggling to see how roses and sunsets have anything to do with leaping back in time, but I have to trust him. After all, he's experienced at this sort of thing. He's my only ticket out of Cortland. So if it's a rose he wants, I'll set the world record for most roses collected in a single day if I have to.

"The weather definitely complicates things," Orion says. "But there is an old flower shop clear on the other side of town." He draws an imaginary line across the glass. He talks all low and dramatic like he's starting a story. "The answer to our prayers, and to this mission, can be found there." When Orion switches into pretend mode, it's with full commitment.

Seeing the town from this angle reveals how narrowly built it is. Probably four times longer than it is wide. I'm not the best at measuring, but I doubt this mission would be a quick one.

Plot idea: *Boy walks the whole equator, is home in time for supper.*

"That's really far," I say.

"Well we can't go today, Christopher Fritz. You're not dressed for the cold." He ignores me when I point at his shorts. "And we can't tomorrow. Hockey practice." I had forgotten about that. "But on Friday, we march! It'll take literally an hour each way, so dress for it."

He hasn't realized that we'll never make it back in time for my pickup. I wonder about asking if we can just catch a ride to the flower store. But then I remember Orion saying that his aunt can't know about me. Truthfully, I don't really want to meet her either, based on what he has told me. And I'm not sure how Mom would feel about me asking to go flower shopping with our cartoon character of a neighbor boy that she doesn't even know exists. There are questions there I'd rather not have to answer.

"Why don't we use bikes?" I ask. Orion turns to stone.

"What?"

"That green bike in your yard. Mine's probably in our shed somewhere. It'll be way faster if we bike there."

Orion studies his silver, strappy shoes. "That's not an option," he says. He rests his hands on the glass display of a city gone by. "I don't know how to ride."

"I can teach you!" I say. My whole body fuels up with energy. "I taught my sister how to ride, it's so easy." I've been getting shown around and helped so much this week that the idea of helping someone else makes me feel capable again. I hadn't realized I had lost that. "It'll be great," I say as I start drawing over roads on the display. "We can start at home, but then we can practice over here by the library and after—"

"I. Can't. Ride." He has molten tears welling up and the wild horses are back. He is trying to tame them, but his breathing gets real heavy. His face is flushing into an angry, threatening red. Embarrassment doesn't usually look this hot.

"I'm sorry, I didn't—"

With one swift swipe, Orion snatches my library book off the glass and, with a roar, he rips half the pages clean out. He screams as he hurls what's left of the book into the wall and runs out of the library.

I don't see Orion for the rest of the day.

CHAPTER 12

Lemons

MY WILL TO LIVE IS TESTED AT 5:00 THE NEXT morning when Mom hits my door open and flicks the lights on. "Good morning, my Sea Critter!" she sings.

I hide under my sheets, praying that I'll suddenly fall into a coma on the spot. She tosses my new swim shorts at me and dances away to the kitchen, the soundtrack from some musical echoing softly in the hallways.

I had tried to predict how she would react to me telling her that I was going to join a swim team. I figured she would raise her eyebrows and laugh and say, *"You? A swimmer?"* What I didn't expect was to be yanked off the floor in a swirling hug and taken straight away to Walmart to buy swim gear. She nearly broke her tablet screen when she tossed it to the side.

At 5:30, Rhett and his dad pull up on Willoughby Lane in a roaring white truck that I'm worried will wake Oakley. I'm passing milky, color-faded marshmallows back and forth with a spoon when Mom greets Rhett at the door. "Morning, dude," he says with an upward nod toward me. He is way too awake. Mom doesn't ask about his broken arm like I expect her to. Probably something about courtesy and restraint.

I don't know why I feel embarrassed for Mom to meet Rhett. They're chatting about Weston Elementary and I can see that Rhett is far more comfortable with small talk than I am. He's almost eloquent.

I try to hurry out the door, but—of course—pictures.

Mom takes dozens of me alone, first with my swim bag, then without. Then we do some with both me and Rhett standing on the doorstep. Rhett puts his not-broken arm around me like we've been best friends since kindergarten, and I can't help but notice that he smells super clean and lemony. And nice. I know it makes Mom proud to see me doing something besides sitting in my room burying myself in words and pictures. She thanks Rhett for talking me into this, which I sneer at.

After the longest photo shoot in the history of film, we race over to Rhett's white truck rumbling softly on a mostly slumbering Willoughby Lane. I find space in the back between two Oakley-style booster seats while Rhett buckles up in front.

"Sorry 'bout the mess, kiddo," Mr. Robbins says as we pull away. "Five-year-old twins are a special kind of messy."

There are cracker crumbs mashed in the cup holders and a dark splatter on the floor where juice was probably spilled.

Makes me smile to remember when it was Oakley making similar messes not too long ago. But then I remember that it was Dad who was usually picking it up.

Plot idea: *Boy afraid of own reflection breaks every mirror in the universe.*

CHAPTER 13

Extra Grace

MOM SAYS THAT EXPECTATIONS CAN BE the root cause of disappointment. She usually says it when she gets experimental in the kitchen and cooks a crappy meal. But it's me who's feeling it today after my first ever practice with the Cortland Surge Junior Swim Team.

I learned that twenty lengths in a pool is a lot harder than I expected it to be. That, and oxygen is more valuable than gold. I also learned that Rhett might be the most well-liked kid in the history of fifth graders. Not a single second ticked by this morning without Rhett having two or more swimmers in his space. His magnetism reminds me of Orion. But where Orion's energy is playful and energized, Rhett's is confident and strong. If Rhett wasn't Rhett, he'd be Jupiter. Lots of gravity and a signature red that's easy to get caught staring at.

My body is fighting a war this morning. Mr. Tippin is teaching about adverbs, but I can't sit up and focus. Hunger and fatigue are making my eyes flit, and Rhett tells me that this is normal after a morning in the pool.

Plot idea: *Boy gives up on Olympic dreams, eats and naps for the rest of his life.*

It is by divine miracle alone that I manage to stay awake for the whole school day and the five-block walk to the Cortland Community Library. Thursday. Orion's at hockey. And although I'd like to look at our next missions, my body is too tired for any walking or climbing buildings.

"Daily! My guy!" Stormy says as I enter. I wave and head for the new Book of the Day: *Blink.* I admire the lizard-like green cover and pick it up from the display just as Stormy calls out. "Daily, come here quick. Gotta question for you."

I pull up the little kid chair nearby and sit across from Stormy. Her puffy white marshmallow hair betrays her from a distance. She's younger than I first thought. No way she is older than Mom.

"Hi," I say.

"What happened with that book in the local history room yesterday, hmm?" She doesn't ask it in an angry sort of way, but my body floods up with guilt. I don't want to answer this question without Orion here to speak for himself. I bite at my thumbnail. "It's okay," she says, trying to reassure me. "We just need to know."

"Well," I say, stretching the word out. "I accidentally made Orion mad."

Stormy nods an understanding nod.

"He's the one who tore it up?"

"Yeah." I explain to Stormy that Orion had a flare up of embarrassment. I tell her that I should have stopped talking about riding bikes after Orion admitted he hadn't learned how, but I just kept going and pushed him over the line.

"That's nice of you to protect his feelings, but Booker is in charge of his own hands."

"Are we in trouble?" I ask.

Stormy sits back in her chair and folds her hands. She pauses for a moment before shaking her head no. Then she leans in and waves me in close. "Sometimes our friend Orion needs a little extra grace," she says with a wink.

We both lean back.

"So what did you think of *Onwards and Backwards?*" She's smiling again.

Lightning jolts away my swimming fatigue. "Oh, my entire gosh!" I say. "Where do I even begin?"

Stormy and I dissect that story for the next ninety minutes, occasionally pausing so she can help a snotty little kid or inquisitive parent. Mom isn't as tired as usual when she comes to pick me up. And with Mom's permission, Stormy is able to make me my own library card which I use to check out the Book of the Day.

"Now you don't have to borrow a card," Stormy says. I twitch. Somewhere in the world, a preschooler just got caught sneaking chocolate chips.

"Who's have you been using, Critter?"

Tell. Nobody.

"Rhett Robbins let me borrow his card," I say. Stormy catches it. I can see it on her face. I apologize to God for the lie and hope that he'll whisper for Stormy to stay quiet. "Come on, I want to tell you about swimming."

I like the way my Mariners hoodie beams in the evening sunlight, its reflective compass logo smooth to the touch. As I'm telling Mom about my twenty lengths and the water vocabulary I learned, I see someone extra sitting in the car with Oakley. A familiar dusty black ponytail. "Who's that?"

"Oakley has a friend coming over tonight," Mom says while clicking the doors open. "Her name is Kadence."

"Are you kidding me? We have to babysit?" Makes my brain go way back to that Saturday. And that makes me want to key the car.

Plot idea: *Garbage bag home gets invaded by meal worms.*

"Please be my sweet Critter again, Chris. Not a pest."

I sigh so that any astronaut or alien in space can hear me and open the door to a car that's buzzing with second grade melodrama and giggles. I'm thankful for my tired body. I won't be entertaining any of Oakley's friends ever again. Not after last time.

CHAPTER 14

Orbit

O RION GRABS MY ARM AND SNIFFS IT FINGER
to elbow. "You reek of chlorine!" he says.

"Yeah, I joined—"

"You joined the swim team with Rhett. I know." He taps
the imaginary watch on his wrist and points backwards
with two thumbs.

"Right."

My body isn't as tired this afternoon and having Orion
along for my after-school walk speeds things up. I try to
ask about his hockey practice, but he says he doesn't want
to talk about it. When I remember how the poor kid can't
even dribble a basketball with one hand, I think I understand why.

Orion trots ahead of me and avoids every crack in the
sidewalk. Sky blue shorts, spaceship backpack, strappy
shoes. If Orion was a new kid at school, he'd be mistaken

for a second grader, no question. Third tops. There's something funny about him wanting to go back in time.

Orion walks right up to Stormy and apologizes for the damaged book. I never even told him about the talk I had with her yesterday.

"There is something you can do to make up for it." She flips her hair and points to a fat green book rack that is overflowing behind the circulation desk.

"Easiest thing literally ever."

Orion breezes through a tower of chapter books while I put back the picture books. It's really not that hard. I just get tripped up alphabetizing when I get past J. I have to hum the song over and over to make sure I get it right. I'm keen to finish, but when Ava walks into the library, Orion tells Stormy that we are going to take a break and leads me outside, my stack of books abandoned.

Standing on top of the air conditioning unit again, Orion pulls a bright green football out of his backpack and points for me to go long. He heaves the biggest throw he can and almost gets it halfway to me. Big, strong Orion. But I scoop it up and throw it back. My brain goes way back to Oregon when Flint and Calvin and I would play catch for hours and hours. Sometimes Dad would join us. I was never any good, but those afternoons were a special kind of sweet.

"How many missions do we have to do?" I ask.

"I'm not sure. A lot." Orion catches the ball for the first time. "And we have to hurry."

"Why?"

"My aunt is already onto us." He throws again. I wonder if Orion might set a world record for the least accurate thrower of all time. "We probably need to finish by springtime. Perhaps by May. Otherwise my aunt might find our research again like last time."

Orion throws again and the ball lands on the other side of the world. I'm done chasing for now. I sit on my backpack instead of the damp, muddy earth. "Is it weird to not want the weekend?" I ask.

"Yes."

"My sister has a new friend. And she's *so loud*. Like, nonstop singing."

"You should've been an only child. Like me!" Orion claps his hands together.

"No kidding."

"Hey, how high do you think I can throw?" he asks. "Think I can get it on the roof?"

"Please don't," I say. And Orion summons up all eighty-or-so pounds of his mighty self and heaves the football skyward. He's nowhere close to the roof, and my muscles tense up real hard when I see the ball rocketing toward the second story windows. I clench my fists and jaw and listen for the sound of glass, but it doesn't come. In fact, I don't hear anything.

"No way," Orion says. He goes to examine behind one of the trees at the edge of the building. "Christopher Fritz, that window is open." And he's right. This side of the second story is lined with floor-to-ceiling windows that open in the middle. Exactly one window is wide open, inviting in whatever animals or snowfall or footballs might come flying by. I hadn't even noticed the big windows hiding behind the trees. "I want my ball back."

"Orion, no. That's stupid." But stupid me follows stupid Orion as he again climbs on top of the air conditioning unit, the tree branch, and up to the library's midsection ledge. Instead of going towards the entrance like when he took me to the roof, he goes towards the trees and the open window that claimed his football. I follow every step and have to snooze the danger alarm in my head about every three seconds. I might as well get rid of it at this point.

There is a break in the ledge just before the windows that requires a jump. It's not a huge leap, but up here the danger meter on everything has been turned up. Orion, backpack and all, hops effortlessly over and shoots me a proud look. If Orion was an animal today, he wouldn't be his usual puppy self. He'd be a fox. So agile and smooth for being ten feet off the ground.

He does his best secret agent routine as he scans inside the window and waves me along. I watch from the other side of the gap as he wiggles his little body through the window and disappears into the Cortland Community Library. It takes a mini-prayer and several seconds of self-talk, but I make the leap.

"Orion," I whisper from the outside. "Get out of there! I have a bad feeling about this."

"Your little *heart boy feelings* aren't going to get my ball back," he says. He pokes his head out the window opening. "Come on in. I locked the door." I throw my brain alarm in the cerebral garbage and climb through the window.

It's a small and unhurried room that I wouldn't expect to be hiding in a library. There are no books at all. There is a small table with little kid chairs tucked underneath, two small desks, and a whole mess of art supplies. The walls are completely blank, other than having a few nails that must have been used for hanging bulletins boards or something. It feels like an unfinished bedroom without a bed, which is still a more complete bedroom than the one I sleep in. Orion's green football is resting in the corner.

"This is so weird," Orion says. "We're on the adult side. But I don't know what room this is."

"Do you go to the adult side often?"

"Pssh. I know this library literally better than anyone in town." He sits in thought for a moment. "Wait here," he says, and, like a small animal, he scurries out the window and back to the ground. I know what he's doing, but I'm terrified of someone walking in on me in the meantime. My plan is to say that I was just trying to get my ball back if I have to defend myself. God's probably getting used to my lies, so what's one more tally against me anyway?

After about one minute of wishing I could disappear on command, I hear light and uneven steps dancing down the hallway. And humming. It's Orion.

"Are you there?" he whispers at the bottom of the door. I tell him yes and he tries the doorknob. Locked. "Let me in. Twist."

The door opens when I turn it from my side and Orion bolts through. He shuts the door and locks it again.

"Christopher Fritz! This is crazy!" Orion's hands are shaking wildly. Almost violently. "The library got a huge remodel when the children's side was built. We're in the old building right now. Room 325. None of these rooms get used at all!" He starts bouncing.

"Are you sure?"

"I spend more time here than the employees, doofus. Yes, I'm sure. Don't you realize what this means?" He covers his mouth with his hands.

I wonder if kids can be tried for breaking and entering. The law usually takes mercy on kids, because, apparently, they don't know what they're doing. But Orion knows what he's doing. We would need to set a world record as the most persuasive kids ever to convince an officer that we climbed in here by accident. Orion closes his eyes and his body resets.

"It means you don't have to spend all weekend at your house with your sister's new friend," he explains. "It means that I don't have to stay home and get suffocated to death—or worse—by my maniac grouch of an aunt." He grabs my shoulders. "Christopher Fritz. It means that we have a place to keep our research that my aunt won't find." My flame flickers and sparks.

"Did we do this last time?"

"No, my friend. We definitely did not. This is new." He takes out his note card. *Find something worth keeping.* "Forget the rose. This place is what we need." Orion pulls out his white and blue camera and brings me in for a picture. He verbalizes the click.

I love the way Orion is smiling in the picture. It's a real shame I won't get to talk to him after we leap. All the more reason to enjoy him now. Sometimes, he seems like he is stuck in the first half of elementary school. Sometimes, he seems like a magician.

Plot idea: *Boy learns to tie shoes after solving the mysteries of time travel.*

We park ourselves in the tiny chairs and Orion says that we need to keep the door locked and the window open. Easy. And if this place will help ensure that we complete the leap, I'll buy a deadbolt myself if I have to. I tuck my thumbs in my palms and close my eyes.

Dad. Can you hear me? We're coming. I'm going to fix this. We're going to get things back to normal. I'm sorry I've been lying more lately. I know you hate lies. But this is worth it, trust me. We've made some really important progress today, and I'll make sure that we complete the missions as fast as we can. Hang tight. Transmit back.

"We *are* going to help your dad, Christopher Fritz. We're going to get our lives back." And my flame roars with the voice of one hundred lions and lifts me into orbit. "But two things."

"What things?" I ask.

"Thing number one: Nobody can know about Room 325 here. Agreed?"

"Agreed."

"Thing number two," he stashes our picture in his pocket and locks onto me with unyielding icy blue eyes. Wild horses spiraling, frenzied. "Don't believe a single word that Rhett Robbins says."

PART 2

The Inventor

CHAPTER 15

Sunshine

MOM SAYS THAT SIMPLICITY IS THE KEY TO a happy life. So I find it a bit hypocritical that she makes such a fuss over what she calls my now-permanent "*hobo lifestyle.*" I'm perfectly happy with my skyline of cardboard boxes and unopened tubs. And, although the end of January has finally brought all the snow Mom warned us about, I'm content to leave my snow gear packed up in who knows what box. My Mariners hoodie is all I need. If Orion is right about being leap-ready by May, seeing my belongings back in Oregon will be good enough for me.

Plot idea: *Boy abandons civilization, lives among the snow wolves.*

"It's important to me that you do this on your own, Critter," Mom says while drumming on my box towers on a Sunday afternoon. "But I'm not letting you go to school tomorrow smelling like old clothes."

So now I know how to work the washer and dryer myself. And if I learn how to cook a few meals, I'll basically be a fully-functioning adult. Mom says that it's not very adult-like to make signs labeling the clean pile and the dirty pile for the clothes on my bedroom floor. I remind her that it's not very adult-like to blast her favorite music from *The Little Mermaid* in the kitchen, so we're pretty much at a stalemate.

Kadence Atherton is effectively a weekend roommate. A dancing, humming mud puddle. If Kadence was an animal, she'd be a feral piglet with ADHD that never stops oinking. Oakley earned her nickname *"Spiral"* by being so zany and unfocused. Next to Kadence, she looks more like a line segment. Kadence has already broken two of our plates by tripping over imaginary line goblins in the kitchen. "She's sweet and she's learning," Mom tells me as she sweeps up the shards, inexplicably smiling.

Mom acted like she had won the lottery when she found out that Kadence's single mother had a work schedule opposite her own. Now we're stuck with Kadence buzzing and spinning at our house on the weekends, and Oakley spends the early evenings with the Athertons after school. Mom says that staying until 5:00 after work at the high school isn't giving her enough time to get everything done. We were at the Taco Bell drive-through when I suggested that she should just give her students less work so she wouldn't have to grade so much.

She rubbed my shoulder and said, "I'm doing my best, Critter."

Now I get to stay at the library until 6:00 each night. That means more Orion. And since our library is even open on Sundays, it also means that Mom is more understanding on the weekends when I want to *go read somewhere quiet* when Kadence is over. Orion usually joins me in Room 325 after lunch on Saturdays and Sundays. I think I spend more time there than at home.

One Monday, I climbed through the window and was surprised to see Orion setting up Battleship for us to play. He had spent the entire day packing up his rainbow life into his spacey backpack and trotting his things over to our secret space. He said it took more than twenty trips.

"Are you crazy? It's been a blizzard today! School almost got canceled!"

But he shrugged his shoulders, tugged on the leg of his white shorts, and sank each of my ships with surgical execution.

Some days Orion has a new mission, but often he doesn't. "My father is exceptionally calculated, Christopher Fritz. He'll give us our new mission when it's time." Every mission arrives on a lined index card. Every mission ends with a photo.

"What does he do with all the pictures?"

"He looks for what's *essential*," Orion says, smoothly saying that word I've come to dislike.

"So are we going to, like, jump into the pictures or something? To go back in time?"

"We'll leap when we're ready, my impatient and moody friend."

I roll my eyes. I'm sure Dad is ready for us to make the leap. Only he and God know what kind of misery he must be enduring.

One of the special things Orion brought to Room 325 during his move-in was a tiny notebook with a beautiful, red leather cover and a stretchy cord that can hold the whole thing shut. He calls it his photo journal. The pages are blank, but Orion uses the pages to hold all of the mission notecards and their companion photos. One page, one picture. Lots of paperclips. Sometimes when Orion's lost in his coloring, I'll look back through the pictures we've taken.

Just the other day we had a mission to *help someone without being asked.* So, we shoveled the sidewalks on Willoughby Lane clear of all the snow. Boy that was a workout. Poor Orion could barely lift a full shovel with that tiny body of his. Mrs. Howard three doors down caught us from her kitchen window and brought us out some minty hot chocolate as a thank you treat.

When Orion asked her to take our picture, she caught the exact moment we clicked our paper cups together and I accidentally knocked Orion's out of his hand. There's a wide-eyed Orion hopping away from a falling river of molten chocolate to protect his uncovered shins. He laughs every time he sees that picture. And he looks at it a lot.

This week, we had a mission to *buy something you want, but don't need.* Orion took me down to a clothing store a few blocks past the movie theater. He greeted the store clerk Andre by name, a small, portly fellow with a mustache straight from Italy.

"Mr. McBride! How's the old man holding up?" I wondered then if Orion actually knew every single person in Cortland. Seemed a safe bet.

Orion led me to a display in the back of the store full of costumes and crazy hats that were probably kept around for Halloween season. "Something I want, but don't need," he repeated as he browsed. "Christopher Fritz, I know what we need to do." And he didn't even have to say it. We tried on every single outfit in the store that day and dramatically flaunted our costumed selves before the mirrors—posing, dancing, cooing. Knights, astronauts, cheerleaders. It was an afternoon that could only be scripted by the best pretender in the history of kids.

When I burst out of the changing room wearing the unicorn costume, Orion dropped to his knees in a fit of laughter, pounding his hands against the floorboards. I danced in a circle around a gasping Orion who, through his laughter, was pleading, "I can't breathe, I can't breathe!" And that made me dance crazier.

Plot idea: *Best friends learn to freeze time, go to the fair.*

We took so many pictures for the mission card that day. Orion decided on a comically large foam cowboy hat that could hardly fit out the door.

"Clap for me, Andre. Admire me," he said as he modeled the hat for his shrieking, imaginary runway audience.

Orion ran back to the mirror for one last confirmation look before his purchase.

"Sure is nice to hear that boy laughing," Andre said to either himself or to me.

I wanted to ask what he meant, but Orion bounded back too quickly. He unclipped the ten-dollar bill that came with the mission card and wore his behemoth of a hat all the way back to Room 325.

There's something about Orion that I just don't get. He's playful like my old friends Flint and Calvin, and he's full of busyness and motion like Oakley. But he has a way of drawing people towards him. Mom would say, if she met him, that he just *has a certain charm*, and I think she'd be right. Ava asks about him almost every day at school. I think about him almost every hour. Everywhere we go on our missions, people are always giving him this look like they want to take care of him, like Stormy and Andre and Mrs. Howard.

It's getting close to pick-up time for me. Mom will be expecting me back in the children's library. Orion's smile can be seen from space when he cannonballs down into the snowbank under our window, his cocoa-colored hair and golden scarf swirling in the winter wind. That smile. Makes my brain do backflips wondering how he could own a smile like that and still want to go back in time at all.

Plot idea: *Boy gets cut open, but there is no blood. Only sunshine.*

CHAPTER 16

Music Lessons

THE STRANGEST THING ABOUT BEING FRIENDS with Orion McBride is not telling anybody that I'm friends with Orion McBride. That's why it catches me by surprise after breakfast when I open the front door to my grinning, backpack-wearing, animated neighbor. Pink shorts today.

"Good morning, Christopher Fritz."

"What are you doing here? It's Sunday. I'll meet you *you know where* after lunch."

He shakes his head no. "I think we're going to need some extra help for today's mission." He holds up his index card which reads: *Make some music.*

"I don't know how to play music," I say.

"Me neither. But I literally know someone with a sister who likes to sing."

"I'll see you later," I say, shutting the door on him. But he stomps his foot down in the way.

"Hey!" Orion barks. "Do you want to leap back or not?"

I sigh and Orion shows himself in. For the first time since moving, I feel embarrassed about my bedroom and hope that he doesn't ask to see it. He doesn't know that I'm saving my energy for Oregon. He also doesn't know that I have never once mentioned his name to my mom or sister. He's like my secret cartoon companion who just happens to be a time traveling genius. I like it that way.

Mom walks through the living room, enthralled by her tablet and a mug of something toxic and caffeinated. When she finally looks up, she seems barely fazed to see a random boy in all his tie-dye, sunny-smiled glory standing in our living room. "Who's your friend, Critter?"

"Uh, hi, Mom. This is, um, Orion. From school." *Sorry, God.*

They exchange waves as Mom looks him down and up.

"Shorts and sneakers in February. Tough customer," Mom teases.

"We're gonna go play outside," I say quickly.

"Snacks are in the kitchen. Have fun, boys." And just like that, my secret friendship with Orion is out and Mom scoots off to her room, sipping, humming, hardly a care.

Plot idea: *Boy mistakes rocking chair for electric chair.*

"Okay. Where's your sister?" He follows the noise trail of eight-year-old fairy hunters and walks right up to Oakley's room where she is playing with Kadence. Her stuffed toys are scattered strategically and Stardust, for whatever second-grade reason, is spinning slowly on the ceiling fan. Orion sits down beside Oakley as if he already knew which girl she was. Lucky. *Or maybe we've done this before.* "Oakley Fritz," he says.

"Hi?" she says like a question while looking at me.

"I'm Orion. We need your help."

"With what?" Kadence asks.

"Your brother tells me you're a good singer. And we want lessons." He looks back at me with a wink.

"*We?*" I ask from the doorway. A thousand fireflies take flight in my sister as she leaps up, her smile so big it reminds me and the entire planet how many teeth she's lost this year.

"We've done this before, Christopher Fritz. It'll be okay."

I actually enjoy going to music class at school, especially when we do drum circle. What I don't enjoy is giving Oakley power. And now Oakley faces us in the living room holding her battery-dead purple microphone like a pointer. The dining room chairs have been arranged to face her like a classroom and Orion, Kadence, and I have just been enrolled.

Oakley clears her throat. "Good morning, class. Today we are going to learn the *do re mi* stuff." She knows that it starts with do, re, mi, but she makes the rest up and wails up and down scales with Kadence and Orion. The best pretender in the history of kids is all-in. I see pure fascination glowing on his face. He sure loves to play.

After we all try a scale by ourselves, Oakley announces her assessment results. "Kadence: pass. Orion: pass. Chris: huge fail."

"Hah!" Orion laughs with a clap.

"That's crap!" I say standing up. "I can out-sing any of you dorks!" And that's when the game spins away into a high note contest. Orion can sing way higher than I expected, but Kadence can sing above the cloud line. I'm pretty sure Kadence could set a world record for the highest note ever, though it's more of a shrill yelp than anything worth listening to. Which is probably why Mom kicks us all out into the backyard, where a game of Catch Orion immediately starts up. I spectate from the steps. Mom's taking pictures from the kitchen window and I pretend to not see.

"Christopher Isaac Fritz, you renegade!" Orion yells during the pursuit. He swats the girls back with Oakley's foam bat. "Our kingdom is being overrun by pixies and you're just gonna *sit there?*"

He throws the bat in my direction with the same accuracy he throws a football. Looking at the tattered toy, I wonder why it was so easy for Orion to waltz into my house and play like this. I haven't had it in me to play with Oakley since we moved. He does this so naturally. *They love him*, I think. *He's just got that sunshine.*

Plot idea: *Boy adopts a dog from the cat shelter, the dog gets homesick.*

He's pinned down and being tickled to pieces by the second graders. I can hardly understand his words as he chokes out, "Help! Me! Please!"

Plot twist: *Boy adopts the kittens, too.*

I grab Oakley's bat and bound into the fray, ordering the release of the prisoner.

We play in the snow until—for the first time in all of recorded human history—Orion admits that he's cold. Mom prepares some grilled cheese sandwiches for all four of us. Pepper Jack cheese. Dad's favorite. We stuff ourselves silly without a single word and our faces slowly regain their normal color. Mom is pretending to clean the kitchen and she keeps looking over at us. Orion uses his camera to take his obligatory picture of the four of us, and I see Mom sneak some pictures from afar, too.

A question about who is older between Oakley and Kadence turns the conversation to birthdays. It's a bit of a touchy subject for my sister, who has sworn off parties entirely.

"My birthday's on Friday," Orion says.

"What? Are you serious?" I ask. It never occurred to me that a cartoon character could even have a birthday.

"Yeah. I'm turning eleven."

"Critter, let's think of something nice to do for Mr. Orion, yeah?" Mom says. But my brain sets the world record for fastest gift idea ever.

That night, Oakley and I crowd around Mom and her tablet while we search for Orion's present. "I like your friend, Chris. He's cute," Mom says.

"Why would you say that?" I ask, a complete verbal reflex. My temperature goes up by a thousand degrees.

"Because he *is* cute," Oakley says. Mom gives her side a tickle.

"Are you sure he'd like this? I didn't even know this was a thing," Mom says. "Is it because of his name?" I go along with that because she'd never understand in three million years why this is the best gift I could possibly get him. She places the order and I worry out loud about the price. "Critter," she says softly in my ear. "I got to see my son today because of that boy. I'll buy him the moon if he wants that, too."

As hoped, Orion's gift arrives on our doorstep in time. I keep it in my backpack until Friday when I meet Orion in Room 325. I greet him as I twist myself through the library window. He's sitting on the floor with a letter in hand. I recognize the bright, bronzy, block-letter W on the discarded envelope behind him. It's the logo for my school.

"You got a letter from Weston?" I ask.

Orion laughs as he folds it into a tiny square and tucks it into his spacey backpack. He says that the teachers are always begging him to consider enrolling because he would make their test scores skyrocket. They ask every single week. Sounds about right. I bet a time-traveling eleven-year-old has a much better grip on division than I do. But I have more important things on my mind today.

"Want to go to the roof?" I ask.

Ever agreeable and adventurous, Orion leads the way up and we sit once again on the roof of the Cortland Community Library, legs dangling, buttery popcorn smell in the air activating my stomach.

"Does eleven feel different than ten?" I ask.

"The numbers never feel different," he says. I have to agree with that.

"I got you something," I say as I unzip my backpack. I take out a small black box and place it on Orion's lap. "Happy birthday."

Orion slides the lid off the box and pulls out an intricate and decorative paper that reads *Star Certificate*. "Christopher Fritz, are you kidding me?" he asks with a delighted laugh. Orion searches the rest of the box. A star chart, a letter, a sky atlas, among other things.

"I got you a star!"

"And you even named it after me," Orion says, holding up the certificate. "*Light of Orion.*" He leans back and searches upward. The sunset still masks all the stars, but he's staring as if he knows exactly where in the universe his star is behind our evening apricot sky.

"I wanted to get you something that you could keep after we leap back," I say. "Now you can own the stars like that guy in *The Little Prince*," I say.

"If I'm not mistaken, he had five hundred million."

"Hey, it's a start." Orion thanks me for the star. And even though we didn't do a mission today, Orion takes out his camera and documents not only us, but also his star box. But then his smile fades and he falls quiet.

I can't see the wild horses in his eyes. Just rocking ocean waves at the moment. He's lost in his own head, just staring. He does this sometimes. He'll look out past the horizon and go far, far away. Beyond Cortland. Beyond the mountain scape. Beyond us. I'm not even sure he knows where.

"Are you doing anything special tonight for your birthday?" I ask.

"Christopher Fritz," he says, eyes skyward, "this is all I wanted to do today."

CHAPTER 17

Cursive

I IMAGINE DUNKING MR. TIPPIN'S CREAM COL-
ored tie into a mug of hot chocolate. Rhett wanted to
talk to me at recess, so sitting here instead for my third
conference has me more than a little tilted.

Plot idea: *Boy hides from police officer in the officer's coffee mug.*

Mr. Tippin is tapping his pen as he browses my blue
folder of *calibrated data.* I'm trying to look at anything else
besides his disappointed expression. The two diplomas
framed behind his desk. The perfect hand-drawn calendar
on the white board. The matching graphite point of every
pencil in the cup on his desk. Mom would say that Mr.
Tippin is super straitlaced, and I think she'd be right.

"Chris, I'm a little concerned," Mr. Tippin says. He's
massaging one hand with the other. "Let's commit to honesty. Honesty begets growth." I like to imagine that every

time Mr. Tippin uses one of his character-building catch phrases, an angel loses its wings. Pretty much all of Heaven is probably grounded by now. "How do you feel about our current math unit?"

"It's okay."

"Yesterday's assessment caught my attention. In questions concerning expanded place value, subtracting fractions, and using the coordinate plane, you answered three correctly. Out of twenty." He places yesterday's test in front of me, marked to bits with red pen.

"Oh."

"I can see you didn't double check your work," he says, pointing through my assessment with a pencil so sharp it might be considered a lethal weapon. "And your reading is becoming a red flag as well."

"I read all the time! I've started and finished like two books this week."

"But your reading log is empty, Chris. Look."

"But I'm reading!"

"Success is a job *fully* done, young man," he says. Sometimes his relentless professionalism makes me want to stick my tongue in the pencil sharpener. "I love seeing you with a story in your hands. I love the energy you bring to your team's book discussions. But you have to see a job through to completion."

An unintended eye roll escapes me. "Chris, what's going on? I expected your performance to improve after settling down in Cortland. It seems like the opposite is happening."

I wonder how often teachers mistake the truth for an excuse. I can't imagine that Mr. Tippin would let me slide if I told him that I'm planning to travel back in time with my magician neighbor to prevent this move from ever happening. But that is the truth, so reading logs and fraction worksheets have not been high on my priority list. My priority list has only one entry: get Dad back. Everything else is gravel under my shoes.

"I'm just really tired after swimming every morning," I say. It's part-truth, but it's mostly a lie. I've gotten stronger. I've actually grown to enjoy the early morning routine, especially breakfast with Rhett. Twice a week, Mom makes real hot breakfast as a way to thank the Robbins family for chauffeuring me around so much. Mom and Mr. Robbins shoot the breeze over a pot of coffee while Rhett and I get fat on spicy breakfast burritos and chocolate milk. His arm will be healed by March, so he says he wants to *carb up* for when he can get back in the water.

"If swimming is going to affect your schoolwork, we may need to have a meeting about how much you can handle, Chris."

Somewhere in the world, a bull sees red. I'm not letting Mr. Tippin take away those mornings.

"I can do it. Really."

"Well, please let me know if I can help. That's my job." Conference adjourned.

For the first time, I won't be in Mr. Tippin's WIN group starting today. The WIN groups are shifting from writing to math, so I'm not in the smart group anymore. The teachers say that there is no smart group, and every student is getting *the precise instruction necessary.* But all the kids know better. Kids keep score, and everybody knows it.

As I gather my math materials from my desk, Ava asks the same question she asks every single day: "How's Orion doing?" Her question has become as routine as my morning swims and checking out the Book of the Day. It's something I can always count on. And it always reminds me of what Orion said.

Tell. Nobody.

"I don't know," I answer for the ten billionth time with a shrug. "We're not really friends, you know. Just neighbors." I wonder when I became such an enemy of the truth. I'm sure God's wondering the same thing.

"Really?" she asks. "I see you two at the library all the time and I—"

"Wait," I interrupt. "The nons? We're not supposed to talk about people out of the room." Ava rolls her eyes and I head for the door to join my non-smart-kid WIN group.

I follow a few classmates to Mrs. Correy's room across the hall. The desks and chairs are familiar, but that's about it. There are plants potted in the windows and some hanging from the ceiling, and there's a rabbit named Rubble in a cage near the sink stinking up the whole place. Only window light. I think this might be Mrs. Correy's way of saying she'd rather be outside than with a bunch of sweaty kids. We join up in the middle of this dim, earthy, symmetrical classroom and pick a desk.

Mrs. Correy's voice is nasally as she explains the math worksheet. More fractions. More parts of a whole Cortland experience I can't wait to ditch. She's clearly struggling with allergies today, which makes me wonder why she has so much outdoor stuff in her indoor classroom. I wonder which classroom would break my spirit first: Mr. Tippin's Vacant Void of Professionalism, or Mrs. Correy's Indoor Jungle Safari. Either one makes me want to teleport to Room 325 with Orion.

And that's when I notice the nameplate on the desk I'm sitting at.

Plot idea: *Boy meets polar bear in downtown Miami.*

Bold, beautiful, blue cursive letters spell out a familiar name: Orion McBride.

"Why does Orion have a desk here?" I ask, interrupting Mrs. Correy's instruction. She's blanked. "He said that he's homeschooled."

"Orion says a lot of stupid crap," a boy named Daniel says with his eyebrows high. The group laughs. And their laughter scratches me in a way that goes way down deep.

"Fifth graders," Mrs. Correy says, ending the moment. "Mr. McBride is not in the room, and we have three nons that we follow at all times. Do we need to review them?" Silence. "Thank you. Take a look at number one."

Somewhere in the world, a dam cracks.

CHAPTER 18

Tempest

I WALK STRAIGHT DOWN THE MIDDLE OF THE road from Weston Elementary to Willoughby Lane. I'm thankful that it's not Thursday. I've been practicing in my head all afternoon how I'm going to ask Orion about his desk in Mrs. Correy's room. I want to line up the words just right. He's so crafty and loose when he talks that sometimes it's hard to pin him down.

From a distance, I can see Orion sitting on his stoop and leaning back against his front door. No car with Arizona plates. No scarf. But he's wearing a green helmet and elbow pads and is virtually motionless. I wonder how many people have driven by and were worried about some sorry kid passed out on his own doorstep.

"Hi," I say as I approach him. He doesn't even move. Not even eye contact.

"Before we go to the library, will you help me with

something?" he asks, staring into the universe somewhere beyond me. He holds up his mission index card for me to read: *Learn something new.* Orion holds air in his cheeks for several seconds. "Will you teach me how to ride a bike?"

"Oh my entire gosh, Orion! Yes!"

Plot idea: *Boy discovers a new planet, trades discovery rights for cotton candy.*

Even though the yards of Willoughby Lane have enough snow for a full parade of snowmen, the streets are mostly clear and dry. This might be the only day in February we could do this. If Orion was an animal today, he'd be a wounded kitten who is afraid of a water gun. He swings one leg over his bike, mirroring how I sit on mine. He hasn't even sat down yet and he already looks like he'd rather sell an arm than do this.

"Okay. Just walk the bike forward. Hands on the bars." He's kind of awkward at it, but this step is *idiot proof,* as Dad would say. We waddle with our bikes across Willoughby Lane back and forth a few times, tires ticking. "Great. Now I want you to hold on tight with your hands. Yeah, right there. And sit down."

Orion shivers, maybe because of the orange shorts.

"Now you're gonna push off the ground with both feet. You'll go forward a bit like this, then put your feet on the ground to stop." I model it for him twice. Orion nearly falls over the first time. And the second time. But by the third time he looks steadier. And the fourth is even better. "Are you okay, Orion? Your shaking is, like, out of control."

"Let's just do this," he bites.

"Last step. This time you're going to do the same thing. Hold tight and push off. But instead of stopping yourself with your feet, put your feet on the pedals and go! It'll feel unsteady at first, but you have to trust your feet."

Orion is tense. His wild horses are bucking.

"Walk behind me?" he asks.

"Ready. Set. Push." Orion launches and his silver, strappy shoes flail in all sorts of crazy directions trying to land themselves on the pedals, but he goes tumbling to the pavement before he gets five feet down the road. He lies still, helmet resting on the street.

"Are you okay?" I ask, kneeling down by him. He shakes his head no. I can tell he's trying not to cry. "Come on, let's try again." And I lift him to his feet.

"I don't think I can do it," he whimpers. He sounds like a toddler.

"Yes you can. If you can solve time travel, you can ride a bike. You're *untouchable*."

Orion resets. He tightens his grip on the handlebars as I help balance the back tire.

"Ready. Set. Push!"

Orion launches again and this time his feet find the pedals right away. His body wobbles this way and that, but he's trying to pedal too fast. His shoes zip wildly in circles around the pedals. Just when it looks like Orion is going to find his balance, the bike teeters and he bails off into his driveway, landing on his hands. Again, he stays down.

"You're so close!"

"I can't do it." He's really choking up and he won't look up at me.

"One more try," I say. Orion punches the pavement with a closed fist.

"I. Can't. Do it!" And every volcano on the planet erupts at the same time. Orion punches the ground again and screams into the road until his lungs hit empty. He rips his helmet off and heaves it across the street, hitting a parked car. There's a tempest in his eyes. Absolute chaos. It's so much bigger and darker than anything I've ever seen in him.

Orion drags his bike away from me by the handlebars, tightens, spins, and pulls the bike into orbit around himself. One revolution. Two. The bike whirls through the afternoon air like a comet before violently smashing into the wall of his house. Pure carnage. Wild horses run riot.

The bike frame is all sorts of misshapen. Orion kicks it repeatedly as one tire spins and spins and spins for mercy under a newly formed crater in the house siding.

"Mission failed," he says from his doorway. He slams himself inside.

I collect Orion's helmet and leave.

CHAPTER 19

Sequence

"**B**OOKER DID WHAT TO HIS BIKE?" STORMY asks, eyes as wide as a donut hole. She's the only person I can talk to about it. Mom would probably file a restraining order against Orion. Rhett would just laugh. And I even wondered about telling his Aunt Lillian, but I'm not willing to jeopardize our research and my chance to get Dad back. Orion said she can't know about me. That, and she'd probably try to poison me or feed me to a nest of vipers or something.

I've already helped Stormy re-shelf the picture books. I'm sitting on the other side of her curvy desk in a yellow chair that is probably meant for a kindergartner. She's brought out the candy jar from her office because *something seems amiss*. I'm on my third Reece's.

"It was crazy. He just grabbed it like a sack of potatoes and flung it. It did some real damage," I explain.

"And all because he fell?"

"Yeah. I mean, he was already kind of pouty when I got there, but then he just lost it." Stormy holds the candy jar open to me again, but this time I decline.

"Daily, that reminds me a lot of what happened with my book. You said he got mad and tore it up."

"I thought of that, too," I say. "I just don't get it. He can be so happy and fun to be around. He's like my best friend." Stormy nods along with me. "But then other times he just, I don't know. He detonates." I nuke the world with my hands. "He gets *so angry*. And he destroys stuff." My brain knows what words to say, but my heart doesn't want to say them. My eyes connect with Stormy's and I err on the side of trust. "It scares me when he loses it."

Plot idea: *Boy brings his own shadow to life with his breath.*

"Stormy, you said something after Orion ripped up that book." She sneaks some candy for herself. "You said he needs grace. What does that mean?"

"Great question, Daily." Stormy clears her throat from the chocolate. "We have to remember that everybody is fighting something in here." She points to her heart. Then to mine. "If we seek to understand that in each other, we can be each other's teammates instead of obstacles."

"Seek to understand," I repeat. Somewhere in the world, a searcher just won a game of hide and seek.

I hurry off to the shelves with my brain screaming one title over and over. I'm pleased to find not just one, but *five* copies of *The Little Prince* in the S section. Stormy checks it out and slips the return receipt in the front cover. "Orion loves this book. It's like the Bible to him," I say.

"I like the way you think, my friend. Get to know him through a beloved book."

"I've actually read it once already, but I didn't really understand it." I flip through the pages as my brain recalls the illustrations and scenes from my first read. The rose, the vain man, the fox. The book fits snugly in the pocket of my Mariners hoodie.

"What didn't you understand?"

I tell her that it didn't feel much like a story as she flips her marshmallow hair out of her eyes. She leans in. I explain that stories are supposed to have a beginning, middle, and end. But when I read *The Little Prince,* it just felt like a bunch of tiny moments strung together. It made my brain do somersaults trying to figure out what was important. "The sequence was all wacky to me," I say.

Stormy claps her hands twice. "Daily! Doesn't that sound a little bit like real life?"

CHAPTER 20

Belly Up

I F THERE WAS A WORLD RECORD FOR THE MOST scrambled day of all time, this might be it. I'm trying to tune out the sounds of giggles and squeals from Mom's studio chair. The one that says *Boss Lady* on the back. I'm trying to pretend I'm interested in this yearbook that is as old as me. But it's no use.

This was supposed to be my special day with Mom. Just the two of us for the first time since the move. She was going to show me her classroom at Cortland High School and teach me how to use one of the real cameras. She said she "*just needed an hour or so in the grinder*," even though it's a no-school Friday.

Oakley and Kadence weren't supposed to be here. They weren't supposed to be vandalizing every single shred of paper with peanut buttery fingerprints and markers. Flowers and spelling words. Motion and chaos. Oakley and Kadence. Ms. Atherton had a big day planned for the two girls, but that got derailed by an animal emergency. So there went my special afternoon with Mom.

Orion wasn't supposed to be here either. Call it lucky timing, I think. We still haven't really talked since the whole *"mission failed"* incident, but he seems to be past that now. Besides, any day with Orion is a good day to me. Lillian and Orion zipped up on Willoughby Lane just as we were all heading to the car. A few introductions and some exchanged phone numbers later, and Orion is now the subject of a second-grade photo shoot.

He's got a soccer ball in one hand and a science beaker in the other. Him paying attention to the halflings rather than me makes me want to burst. I tuck my thumbs into my fists and try to transmit to him, but he's all swallowed up by play. Chirpy, cheery Orion. Always busy.

"Chris, come here!" Oakley says from behind the lens of a student camera. "It's crime scene pictures now. We need somebody to be the bad guy." Mom smiles from her desk. Type, click, type.

I sigh so that everybody in the room hears and I shake my head big and slow. Orion walks right up to me and tries to yank me out of the chair.

"Come on, Christopher Fritz. It's fun!" But I'm stuck to my spot. And actually, it's pretty easy to stay stuck with Orion tugging. He's too little to pull me anywhere. I wouldn't be surprised if Kadence could beat him in an arm wrestling contest.

"Please, Chris?" Oakley begs.

"No," I say, pretending to be absorbed by the yearbook in my lap. "I don't like pictures."

Plot idea: *Boy attends animal show; announces how much he dislikes animals.*

Mom and Orion shoot me the same look at the same time. Sad in the eyes, surprise in the face. *Smooth, Chris,* I think.

"Orion, do you want to go explore the school?" I ask. Anything to pry him away from the girls and from this moment that I've sullied with my words.

"Abso-yes-o-lutely!" Orion says with that sunny smile. I let him pull me from the chair. Mom tells us to not go in any doors or up any stairs, and we promise we won't. Orion halts and spins dramatically at the door. "Oakley Fritz. Kadence Atherton. Amanda Fritz," he calls out, a wave of steely seriousness overtaking him. "Goodbye!" He salutes. The girls all laugh and Mom waves as he scurries into the hallway

As I shut the door, I hear Kadence say to Oakley, "Your brother is a real whiner." And it takes everything I've got to not set a world record for the loudest scream of all time.

Orion has gone into total airplane mode. He's gallop-running up and down the wide hallway, arms fully out. I was hoping he'd be able to talk, but he's stuck in play mode. Almost forcefully so. I still want to know why he has a desk in Mrs. Correy's room. It has been eating away at me for days. And now I have questions about his aunt, too.

Today was the first time I'd ever seen her face. And, to my uncomfortable surprise, she didn't look like I expected. I knew she wasn't *really* a screeching harpy or a chimera with an ax tail, despite Orion's overuse of the word "literally." I wasn't seriously expecting snakes for hair or purple gunk dripping soundlessly from a child-eating maw. But I was still surprised to see that she looked soft and, to be honest, kind. Probably a little older than Mom.

What really threw me for a loop was that Orion was so calm in her presence. Placid, even. I thought he'd turn into a dead sprint after getting out of the car to get away from her. But maybe he just knows how to play it cool to give her the slip.

Airplane Orion flicks each locker that has a yellow sign taped to it. The signs all say *Cortland Cougars!* and recognize students for extra activities and achievements. Bailey: indoor track. Max: student council. Victoria: basketball *and* 4-H.

Makes me wonder about what our signs would say. Chris: swim team. Oakley: worst grades in the history of schooling. Orion: time-traveling genius. Makes me smile to think of that. And then I smile even bigger when I remember that if Orion gets credit for solving time travel, I won't ever get a *Cortland Cougars!* sign at all.

"Look!" Orion says with a point of his finger.

A huge letter C hangs from a high ceiling over dozens of lunch tables. It's gold and frilly, and it's strung up with shiny blue rope. Orion is pretending to take swings at it with a fake bat, even though it's probably twenty feet above us.

"C is for *Cortland!*" Orion sings.

"C is for *cougars?*" I suggest.

"C is for *come on!*" he says. And Orion runs and jumps feet-first onto one of the lunch tables, eyeing upward at the big C. "I love this school," he says. He daydreams out loud about going to a school with giant piñatas and his very own locker.

"You could come to public school!" I say, failing to play it cool. "We could come here together someday, right?"

Orion laughs, eyes still upward. "You're a funny boy, Christopher Fritz." But I don't get what about that is funny.

Orion lets himself fall to his butt on the table and lies down on his back. He clumps up his scarf for a pillow and locks his fingers over his belly. Ever since he drove up with his aunt, Orion has been a tornado of playful energy. Looks like tiredness is catching up with him. It's almost like he's slowing down to normal-person speed, which is something I've never witnessed firsthand.

And then I catch it. Just a glimpse. But he looks, for just one small moment, not so much like a time-traveling mastermind. Just a regular eleven-year-old kid.

Plot idea: *Boy catches photograph of the caffeinated hummingbird at rest.*

C is for *curious.*

I wonder if it's even worth it to ask Orion my questions. Even if it is, I'm not sure how I'd ask. He's so smooth when it comes to conversation. Makes it hard to keep up sometimes.

Mr. Tippin says that it's a *"prosocial habit"* to give people *the benefit of the doubt.* To trust their positive intent. I wonder what Orion's positive intent might be. Maybe he has a desk at Weston because he guest teaches from time to time. And that eruption with his bike? Maybe it was just one of those cloudy emotional days. Mom says we all have them. Even the boy made of sunshine must have cloudy days, too.

C is for *cloudy.*

I need to let it go. Orion is the only person who can help me get Dad back. I'm taking no risks with him. Ever since our first mission, he's been a real friend to me. A best friend. What kind of best friend would I be if I repaid his kindness and wit with prying mistrust? Maybe I'll ask my questions someday. But not today.

C is for *concede.*

"Hey, Christopher Fritz," Orion says softly with his eyes closed. Still belly up on the table. "Thanks for getting my helmet the other day. I found it in my backyard."

"Sure thing," I say. And my heart skips forward. Here I was thinking that this topic would be off-limits, and then he brings it up first.

"But that whole moment with my bike?" he starts. He opens one eye at me. "I'm sorry I did that. And I'd rather not talk about it. Okay?" It's like he pulled the subject straight out of my brain and crumpled it up and tossed it out.

"Okay," I say reflexively.

C is for so, so, so, so *curious.*

It's just like the time he ruined the library book. Total outburst one day. Forward apology the next. He wasn't asked for an apology either time, he just came out and gave one. If I know anything about Orion, it's that he's the most unpredictable kid of all time. I feel even more at a loss for words now, so I take my best stab at a safe topic.

"I have my first swim invitational tomorrow," I say. "It's over in Darton."

Orion springs up from the table into his puppy stance. "You're going to *Darton?*" he asks. I nod. "You're literally going to waste an entire Saturday? For *swimming?*"

"There are only four invitationals," I say, backpedaling. "And the second one is here in Cortland. No travel!" Orion puts his face in both hands and shakes his head. "You can come watch! Rhett says that during the home meet—"

"You know, you talk about Rhett a lot," Orion interrupts.

"What? No, I don't," I protest.

"Yeah, you do. Like, *a lot.*"

"I'm sorry," I say. "Rhett's my friend. And I just thought—"

"Well I don't want to hear about *Rhett Robbins,*" Orion snaps, mocking his name. He hops off the table and starts walking away. "I'll do the mission alone tomorrow. Go be with your fish friends."

I call his name and try to apologize, but he shoos away my words with one wave. "I want to go take some more pictures," he says. And he's gone.

And that's just how the world seems to work for me. I smack the lunch table and the sound echoes off the brick walls behind me. I bury my face in my arms. *Mission failed yet again.* At least that's what it feels like.

I can burn through all my energy trying to play it safe and soft with my words. But then, like clockwork, I muck something up. I always end up feeling like I need to apologize, and I'm not even sure what for. I wish somebody would give *me* the benefit of the doubt one of these days.

Plot idea: *The Alphabet Book of Failure. C is for Christopher.*

CHAPTER 21

Crowning Achievement

MOM SAYS THAT I LIVE A SHELTERED LIFE. That I don't challenge myself to grow very much. I wish she had been there today to see how wrong that is. How proud of me my teammates and coach were after I finished my first swimming invitational with the Junior Surge.

I'm glad it wasn't a real competition. My relay team took next-to-last in both heats, and the best I did in my solo events was fifth. "But nobody's keeping track," Rhett said with a wink. I imagined Dad sitting on the bleachers watching me. I could see the thumbs up he would have given me at the end of one of my events. I gave one back to nobody.

Plot idea: *Boy conquers entire continent, discovers that the population is zero.*

I spent a lot of the day thinking about Orion. How he was so upset about this trip to Darton. How he told me to *go be with my fish friends*. Made it hard to want to pack my swim bag this morning. I hope his mission was a success today. I'll ask him about his new photos as soon as I get the chance. But for now, I'm stuck here.

One of the few good things about life on Willoughby Lane is that I almost never have to ride a school bus, which is basically a vomit-inducing sweat lodge on six wheels. This is the first day I've been on a bus since Oakley and I got pulled out of school in Oregon. It's a three-hour ride back to Cortland, and most of the Junior Surge are either zonked out on the floor or, like Rhett beside me, listening to music.

Rhett has streaks of ashy black hair where his cardinal red is starting to fade, and he'll be able to take his arm sling off soon. He snapped a pencil in frustration yesterday during math because his only good hand wasn't cooperating. Makes me feel bad for him.

I'm surprised that Rhett chose to sit beside me both ways today, given that he's friends with pretty much the entire school. Makes me wonder things. He's tracing his embroidered last name on his swim bag with one finger when he catches me staring at his hair, so I pretend that I'm counting reflector posts along the roadside. I flinch when Rhett taps my knee.

"Dude, it's Valentine's Day on Monday. You doing anything special?" He holds the word "special" for a full hundred days. I'm taken aback by his question.

"No. I don't really like Valentine's day," I say. Liam and Patrick turn around in their seat to listen in.

"But I know someone who likes you," Rhett says in a singsong, Oakleyish way. My shoulders lock up and my lips seal shut. Makes my brain wonder if I would survive a jump out of this window. I could hitchhike home, or anywhere else on the planet away from this conversation. Under a boulder or in a bonfire would be great.

"Who?" Patrick blurts.

"Dude. Ava Mayfield," Rhett says. He squeezes my shoulder. "She's *crazy* about Fritzy."

"That's not true," I say.

"Are you kidding!" Rhett now has the attention of all of our seat neighbors. "Dude, sometimes during silent reading, she just stares at you for, like, minutes at a time."

"Her and her friends point at you when you read at recess, too," Liam adds. "It's pretty obvious. Why do you read so much anyway?" Annoyance kicks my embarrassment out of the way.

I try to explain that I am planning on moving again soon, and it would make me sad to make close friends, only to lose them right away. Mostly a lie, but whatever. Rhett teases that I use all my attention for reading and have none left for girls. All seven billion people on Earth snicker. Makes me want to shoot lasers out of my eye sockets.

"I don't think she likes me," I protest. "I think she likes my neighbor, Orion." The boys all share looks. "No, really! She asks about him almost every day. It's kind of annoying."

Rhett puts his head in his free hand and sighs. "I'm so sick of that kid," he says slowly. "I'm glad he's gone." Somewhere in the world, a town loses power.

"Why don't you like him?" I ask. I wonder about yesterday when Orion mocked Rhett's name. These two sure have problems. Orion always attracts such a warm fondness from others. I know he can have his moody moments, but what Rhett just said sounded harsh. That felt like a language my brain doesn't understand.

"Well he ruined my swim season for starters," he says, pointing to his broken arm. My brain tries to backflip straight out of my head as I recall Rhett's explanation of the injury.

I got into a little fight.

"Orion broke your arm?" I ask way too loudly. "You got into a fight with *Orion McBride*?"

My heart stops pumping blood. There's simply no way. I look to the boys who are listening, but nobody is denying it. I picture color-splashed Orion. The one that takes pictures and tries on costumes and re-shelves Stormy's books at world record speed. *Orion would never.*

But then I remember there's another Orion. The one who destroys property and rips up books and screams as if to tear down the sky. "He's so little," I say in his defense. "There's no way!"

"Oh my God, it was nuts!" Patrick says. "It was at recess. Something happened with Ava and Orion, and Ava started crying." He uses his hands and tiny finger-people to tell the story. "But then Ava said something about Orion's dad and Orion turned into a freakin' tornado and he smacked her face real good," he says while thwacking the air. "Then Rhett ran in and tried to stop him and, yeah." He points to Rhett's arm. "It took *three* teachers to carry Orion back into the school. And he was screaming and thrashing and crying something fiercer than heck!"

It hurts double to hear this story. One part because I feel bad for both boys. The second part because of how cheerfully Patrick did the retelling.

Here I thought Orion was a homeschooler. My own secret genius companion. But now I know he is a Weston kid with a reputation more busted to bits than Rhett's arm. It's really no wonder he lied about it.

"Is that all true?" I ask Rhett.

"He bit me, bruised a rib, and broke my arm" He massages his side. "The little brat stomped on me eight times before Mrs. Correy grabbed him."

"He got the longest suspension in school history," Daniel says, as if that's a glorious crowning achievement worth celebrating.

"Guys," Liam softly says, "we shouldn't be talking about him. The nons?"

"The nons are a load of crap," Rhett says, except he uses a tougher word than *crap*. "And so is Orion McSpaz. He's a liar and a freak."

Plot idea: *Little Red Riding Boy accidentally befriends the wolf.*

I don't say much for the rest of the ride home. Nobody does. My brain isn't able to untangle these newfound knots, so I go back to counting the reflector posts.

I wonder if they could invent band-aids for when you're bleeding something other than blood. Apply directly to the spirit. I lean against the seat to feel the rhythm of the road, and I wonder for a long, long while if it's Rhett or Orion who hurt my heart more today.

CHAPTER 22

Batteries

P LOT IDEA: *BOY RUINS EVERYTHING FOR EVERY-body in the entire world because he exists.*

"I said no!" The walls rattle as my door slams shut. I throw myself onto my bed and bury my face in a pillow, praying that I can pass out from oxygen loss in the next five seconds. Mom denies me.

"Christopher, stop." She yanks me up by the shirt and grabs my shoulders. "What has gotten into you? Why won't you talk to your father?"

"I'm not talking to him until we're back in Oregon." She kneels next to my bed.

"We're not going back, Chris. This is home now."

"No. I *am* going back." My lungs are working harder than when I swim.

"Chris, look at me." I obey. "Cortland is our home. You need to unpack all of your things and join us in this house.

We can't change what happened."

"Yes I can, Mom. I'll prove it. I'm going to fix everything. And me and Dad are going to the Mariners game." Orion would have me sacrificed to a volcano if he knew what I just said.

Mom rests her eyes and folds her hands the way she did back when we were churchgoers. She sighs.

"It feels like I'm the only one here who still cares about Dad," I say as I cross my arms.

"You're the only one here who won't talk to him, Chris." She takes my hands in hers, and a scream inside me is fighting to be released. "He's been working as hard as he can to earn calling privileges. If you care about him so much, he'd really like to hear you say that."

"Why do you care if I talk to him?" My voice cracks under my shouting. "You and Oakley are getting along just fine without Dad here!" I push over two stacks of boxes on my way out. *Tumble, tumble, shatter.* I bet our pictures of Dad were in there. It's not like they're taking up any wall space.

I retreat to the dining room table and throw my head under my arms. Oakley is stringing beads in the living room and I can feel her pathetic, gnat-like stare as Mom's hands slam the table.

"You think we're fine, Chris? You think we're fine without Shaun here?" I'm ice. I'm ice that cannot be melted by her fiery excuses. "I get up every day and put in a shift as the world's worst teacher before coming home to be the world's worst mother. And you think I'm fine?" My icy core begins to melt. "High schoolers are tough, Chris. Teaching is tough. And I'm struggling. And I want to take away your struggle *so badly*. And I miss Shaun every second of every day.

"I wish he was here instead of you," I stab.

"I know you do," she says. I'm slain. "But right now, this family is all we've got." My useless heart takes over and I have to breathe faster to keep from crying. "And I'm going to get up every morning and fight for you, and fight for your sister. Because that's all I can do." I cover my ears and seal my eyes closed. "I really wish you'd try to fight for us, too."

Oakley leaves her beads and Mom scoops her into her lap.

"Come here, Spiral. Sorry about the yelling," Mom whispers to Oakley. Mom looks back to me. "Your sweet sister comes into my room every single night. And every single night she asks for Daddy." They rock gently. I feel sparks inside me flicking. "And we talk about him. We tell stories. And sometimes we cry about him, Chris. Because we miss him, too." Oakley's floodgates open onto Mom's shirt. They rock some more. "And Critter. We also miss you."

"Me?" I ask. "I'm right here."

"You're ignoring me," Oakley pouts.

"Sometimes Oakley will bring me one of the books you made for her, Critter. And we'll read it over and over, and she'll tell me about the illustrations. And she'll tell me how she remembers why you made it." Oakley's crying gets loud. "And you know what she told me just the other night?" Mom's voice eases to a slow whisper. "She said, 'I wish we could adopt Orion so that Chris will come back.'"

Oakley and Mom both look to me with a look I've never seen before. People sitting across a table have never looked so far away.

"Orion is so nice," Oakley says with a tug at her own shirt strings.

"You just like him because he still acts like a little kid," I say.

"I'd rather have him for a brother than you."

And those words take my batteries out.

I excuse myself and head for Oakley's room. I steal Stardust from her bed, rip the ears off, and throw the whole stupid rabbit out the front door.

CHAPTER 23

Restful and Auspicious

H I, DAD. MY THUMBS ARE TUCKED AS I LEAVE
Weston Elementary. *Are you doing okay? I hope
you're doing better than I am. I bet you're thinking the same
thing of me right now. Fresh air has never tasted so rotten.
I'm sorry that I haven't taken your phone calls. But it's for
the greater good. Mom says that it's a good habit to work
with the end in mind. That's what I'm doing. I don't want to
confront Orion about all the stuff I've learned. No need to
upset him. I can't risk this. I can't risk you. I'm coming. I just
need a little more time. Transmit back.*

"Hi, Christopher Fritz!" Orion is sorting through his
trading cards as I reach Willoughby Lane. Grids and piles
of cards encircle him on the concrete. Whatever Orion ate

for lunch, I can see that he wiped at least half of it on his tan shorts. And, along with the fruity, red juice stain around his mouth, he looks like a four-year-old.

"I'm not feeling great today," I lie. "I threw up at school." Orion puffs his cheeks out and makes a gag noise. "I think I'm just going to go to the library and rest in the tree loft."

"Well, there's no mission today anyway," he says. "Get better soon, Christopher Fritz. Science literally needs you!" he says with one finger held up high. He's fixated on his cards again before I even say bye, and I walk the longest two blocks in the history of measurement.

Room 325 is always different without Orion. No noise. No motion. It feels like I'm alone in a friend's bedroom with the game pieces and cards and unfinished drawings all scattered about. I actually like the way Orion deco-rated one of the walls with glow in the dark stars. I had to put some up high because Orion couldn't reach, and it was starting to look like how Oakley used to decorate the Christmas tree. Orion made sure to measure out and stick on a constellation called *Orion's Belt* because, well, because of course he did.

Mom says that it is in moments of calm that we can best have a conversation with God. I wish I had something to say. More than that, I wish I knew he'd hear me among the millions of other conversations he's probably having. I bet Dad's trying to reach him, too. Busy guy. There are so many hurdles that my brain keeps tripping over, and I want to ask for help.

But that's when I see it.

Orion's spacey backpack plopped down and left behind in a small blue chair, just under his constellation. Somewhere in the world, a kid says their first bad word.

God tells me no. Dad tells me no. Orion, in a burst of color and noise, says no. If there was a world record for curious defiance, I could make a serious case right now. I snag Orion's backpack and dig through each of the pockets. Toys. Cookie wrappers. Another copy of *The Little Prince*. I dig until I find a folded paper square. It's the typed letter from Weston Elementary. I double check that I'm alone in Room 325. All clear.

Plot idea: *Museum curator boy weighs temptation after closing.*

I do what my heart says not to.

Orion,

Happy birthday! I hope you are able to enjoy a restful and auspicious milestone day. We still got out the birthday bongos in celebration of you today. Is there, as I expect, a sugar high in your near future? I want that for you.

Thanks again for helping us pilot the new math program. Hopefully, it has been easy for you to navigate. I know your math-savvy brain and I trust that it is all making sense. With state testing just a few weeks out, class time has been busy, and I haven't had the chance to log in and check your progress. Please let me know if you might have any questions.

Have you read anything lately that you liked? Some of

your friends report seeing you at the library often. I'm glad to hear that you are staying busy this winter.

Your classmates and I miss you dearly, Orion. Please let me know if there is anything you need. You're always welcome to come visit.

Your learning community,

Nadine Correy + Fifth Graders

Somewhere in the world, a bird is shot out of formation. Another lie. "Come visit?" I ask to nobody. Only Orion can get suspended for pounding the snot out of somebody and still be a welcome guest to *come visit*. Makes my brain wonder if the swimmers exaggerated what happened on the playground that day.

And then I remember what Orion said about Rhett when we first discovered Room 325: *Don't believe a single word that Rhett Robbins says.* My mental list of questions is starting to get awfully long.

I arrange Orion's letter and backpack as I found them and head for the children's section.

CHAPTER 24

When an Artist Finds His Flow

AFTER RESHELVING ALL OF STORMY'S returned books and dusting off the windowsills and volunteering to vacuum the whole place, Stormy sits me down because *today seems like an emergency candy day.* I'm glad I didn't have to ask.

I sit across from Stormy with Skittles sorted into color piles on top of my new Book of the Day: *The Champion of Everything.* "That must be nice. I'm just the champion of failing people," I say, eyes downward.

"Daily, stop." Stormy says. "What's going on today?"

"Everything I touch turns to dirt." I push a Skittle between my hands like a puck. I don't even care if anybody is eavesdropping. I tell Stormy that Mr. Tippin thinks I'm "*becoming derelict*" because of my missing homework and floundering math data, and Mom wants to put me up for adoption over a stupid toy. "And the worst thing of all," I say through a mouthful of Skittles, "I think my best friend has been lying to me. A lot."

Plot idea: *Entire army defects. Boy soldier is left to fight alone.*

"And you still call him a best friend?" she asks.

"I don't know how to ask Orion about any of this." She smiles when I say his name. "I'm worried he'll go bananas and he might break my arm or something." I cover my face with both hands. "And I don't want to lose my friends again."

"Did you lose friends when you moved here?" I pull at my own hair. It hurts in a way that feels good. So I pull harder.

"I lost my friends way before we moved. It was horrible." A haze surrounds my brain and I feel the world spinning. Stormy taps her fingers a few times on the candy jar and looks to the ceiling as though her next words are hiding just above us.

"Daily, I want to ask you a question." She pulls my arms away from my face. She says that it's a personal question and that she'll understand if I choose not to answer it. I nod. "What happened back in Oregon?"

All of the memories of that night splatter into my headspace like cards and my brain starts to play fifty-two thousand memory pickup. I can see everything. I can hear the ache in Mom's voice from when she said the word *emergency*. I've never explained what happened to someone before. My heart wants to say it all. To shout it. To scream it loud enough for Dad to hear. But my brain wants to run to Room 325 and do all of Orion's missions in a single day so I can whisper it to him instead. And then it would just be another story.

I close my eyes. Tuck my thumbs. And I'm in Oregon.

$$\bullet \quad \bullet \quad \bullet \quad \bullet \quad \bullet$$

Mom says that the rainy Oregon weather makes her feel gloomy. Something about vitamin D and her being addicted to sunlight. But the storms never make me feel that way at all. I find them refreshing. Like the sky is washing away all the misgivings and sins of the day. The smell of rain meeting earth. The sound of droplets drumming on the roof as tiny trails race down my window. Oakley couldn't have picked a better day for a birthday party.

She's eight today. All five of her best friends are here to help her celebrate. It's one of my favorite things when Oakley has friends over. I pretend that it irritates me; that I'd rather pluck off my toenails than read story after story to entertain sugared-up second graders. But it's their eyes. It's the way they look when I make up a scary story, or when Oakley and I show off the books we've made together. It makes me want to write books for the rest of my life if it'll make people smile like that.

The partygoers are watching a movie after a buffet of cupcakes and corndogs. Oakley wanted everything to be green because second grade social status is earned by being the biggest gross out possible. Mom made green sugar cookies and green frosting for the green cupcakes, and even found tricks online for making green ketchup and green milk. It was the exact level of disgusting that makes my sister giddy.

During cupcakes, Oakley asked me to write her a new story to read before bed. And when six little girls are jumping up and down and begging me to create, those are marching orders that I gladly follow.

I crumple up another paper and toss it to the floor. Another unacceptable attempt at illustrating an archer. *Ranger Oakley vs. The Anti-Green Hobgoblins*. I blame my poor illustration on the desk lamp light reflecting off my fingernails. The girls wanted to paint them before dinner. Bright yellow and blue alternating at the end of each finger. I hope I never have to take a lie detector test because I don't want to admit out loud that I kind of like how it looks.

"My man," Dad says as he walks in. "Woah, kiddo! You've been busy." There are nine completed pages on my desk and about a dozen failed pages on the floor. "New story?"

"Oakley and her friends asked for one." I show him the work I've done so far and explain how the story will end. "I think it'll take about five or six more pages." My wrist is cramping up from all the shading and coloring. Dried up markers and stubby, now-useless, crayons are littering my work space.

"Hey, what do you say we take a break from all these crazy girls?" Dad asks. "Go get some wings, watch the game, enjoy some peace and quiet?" It's Saturday. College game day. Dad loves to watch his Huskies. He hardly misses a game during the fall. With Oakley and her friends hogging up the living room TV, he's left looking for options.

Hot wings always sound good. But I've watched football games with Dad before and they take way too long. Even if I take my work with me, Oakley and her guests would probably be asleep by the time we get back. "Thanks, Dad. But I want to finish this for Oakley." He smiles and drums on my back.

"Ahh, yes. When an artist finds his flow, he has to roll with it. I get that. You have your mom's spirit." I dig through my markers to find a pink that still works. "You're an awesome big brother, Chris." Dad flips my bedroom light on the way out, leaving me with just lamp light and imagination to guide my way.

I nearly wet my pants when someone grabs my hand in the middle of the night. "Critter, wake up." Mom sounds stuffy and hurried. I blink away my sleep and my clock reads 11:24. Oakley is crawling under my covers.

"What's going on?" I whisper.

"There's been an emergency. I'm going to get Dad."

"What happened?" I reach for her, but she gently pushes me back against my pillow. I can hardly see Mom's face in the dark of my bedroom. I can't see the tears, but I can hear them.

"I don't know, sweetie. Right now, I need you to look after your sister. The girls are all gone, but Chloe and her mom are going to rest on the couch until I get back." Oakley is clenching tight to my shirt.

"Is Dad okay?"

"Look after your sister, Critter." And she vanishes. Oakley and I do not say a single word, move a single muscle, or dream a single dream.

Mom comes into my room at 6:48 and sits down on the bed. She takes my right hand and Oakley's left.

"Oakley. Christopher." She holds her eyes shut. "I have news. And we are going to have to be strong." She squeezes tight. "Stronger than ever. Starting right now."

* * * * *

Stormy has my hands in hers. Air is hard to hold. I feel like I might pass out right here in the middle of the Cortland Community Library. I am not even bothering to line up the words first. They are just leaking out.

"Instead of going downtown like normal, Dad went over to Remmington. Like, thirty miles away. That's where his old college roommate lives." My voice cracks and Stormy pushes the box of tissues closer. "They were drinking. And the Huskies won, so they were drinking a lot." I wrap my arms around my middle to keep from coming apart. "It was dark. And wet. And he was driving on the wrong side of the road." Stormy moves to my side of the desk and wraps me up. The stars are burning out in the sky one by one with every word I say. "The crash killed two people. A fifteen-year-old kid and his mom."

Stormy holds my hands tight. It's too much. I'm burning up and drowning at the same time. I feel dizzy enough to collapse. "Flint and Calvin weren't allowed to come over anymore. Everybody at school stopped talking to me. They called me *the kid of the killer.*"

"Oh my," Stormy says.

"We knew without Dad's job that we would have to move. The day Dad got sentenced, I made a promise to God that I would never, ever write another book again. I could have stopped everything from happening if I had just gone with him."

Stormy lets me go. She places my pile of green Skittles in one hand and I pat my moist eyes with the cuff of navy-blue Mariners sleeve with the other.

"Look at me," she says. I try to crush the candy in my hand. I want to destroy it. I wonder if this is how Orion felt when he fell off his bike. "When Booker ripped up my library book, you defended him. You tried to tell me it was your fault. But did you damage that book?"

"No."

"Chris, you have a big, beautiful, people-loving heart. And that might be my favorite thing about you. The way you protect others says so much about who you are. But we are all our own main characters."

"What?"

"Your dad made a mistake. And I am so, so sorry that things happened the way they did. But it wasn't your fault." Somewhere in the world, a candle is lit. "Your dad made his own decisions because he is the main character in *his* story. And it affects you, yes siree it does. But *you* are the main character in *your* story. You get to write what happens next." She looks at me like she's seeing into my soul.

I wonder about Orion. I think about how we're going to leap back and rewrite my prologue, not just add a new chapter. I hope and wish and plead and pray with everything I am that Orion knows what he's doing. There are still so many things I want to ask him. But if he can really get me back to that birthday party, I'll overlook anything.

"Thanks for listening to me."

"It wasn't your fault, Chris. Please believe that."

CHAPTER 25

Peer Editing

I LIKE THE WAY THE INK FEELS ON MY ARM AS Rhett marks me up. He may only have one good hand, but he's mastered this job. "Dude, quit wiggling," he says. My left hand holds the heat sheet while my right arm gets tagged with my events, lanes, and heats. Rhett is slow and precise with his penmanship, and I use his sling to help steady myself. Makes me wish I did more events. Unofficial timing and marking swimmers are Rhett's big jobs as the junior manager during invitationals. "Where's your head today?"

"Huh?" I ask.

"You're zoning out. You need to get your head in the game!" He retraces the numbers on my arm with his marker. I wonder if Rhett is going to dye his hair again. His flickering embers of cardinal red are almost fully hidden through thin tangles of black. I kind of miss it.

But Rhett is right about my brain being elsewhere. Truth is that I'm distracted by Orion and the Weston letter. Ever since that bus ride when I learned about the fight, I make sure to not mention Orion with Rhett around. I had seen a different side of Rhett that day. An ugly and unforgettable side. I don't want to see him like that again. I like this Rhett better.

"Sorry," I say. "I'm just seeing who's here." Shame on me for expecting hundreds of shrill fans cheering the Junior Surge onward to glory. The observation deck is about half full, with chatty parents and busy little siblings chasing each other under the bleachers. I kind of get it, though. It's not like I go to my classmates' events and recitals when I hear about them. But it makes me happy to see all of my teammates shout and wave to their own personal cheer sections.

"Hola, Chris!" Oakley shouts from the deck door. Mom and Kadence are behind her. I knew they'd be coming, but my smile still feels as permanent as Rhett's marker as I watch them find empty spots near the diving blocks. I'm even half-glad to see Kadence, which makes me want to throw up in the pool when I realize it.

I scan the crowd one more time. I was hoping Orion would come. I invited him yesterday as I was teaching him to play Egyptian Rat Killer in Room 325, but he groaned, rolled over like an exposed turtle, and told me I was wasting valuable mission time. "The whole thing is done by two o'clock," I had told him. "We'll still have half of the day for a mission." But he abandoned his cards and went to draw instead. Icy silence.

My first event goes better than expected. Had we been actually competing, I would have walked away with my first-ever bronze medal. Coach Robbins says that I have one heck of a backstroke, and Rhett agrees. "I'm proud of you, Chris. Prouder than you know." Coach Robbins says with a clap on my back. "Most improved fish on the squad, that's for dang sure." Mom hears that and pulls me in for a hug.

"Critter, great job! You've become so strong."

"Mermaids are faster," Kadence says, boredom dripping from her voice. Oakley laughs and agrees and says that I'd look good with a mermaid tail.

"Thanks guys," I say. I haven't seen Mom look at me like this in a while. Maybe since the move. I reach for another hug.

"Pictures!" Mom says, and I curse the fact that my next event isn't right away. Mom uses the pool as a backdrop. Then the CMS mural as a backdrop. Then we include Oakley and Kadence. Then we include Rhett and Daniel before I tell her that I've done enough *cheesing* for today. "Chris, you've gotten so skinny!" she says.

"I hope so," I say. "I'm here, like, every day!"

"I know. It's just that you're always hiding in that mangy hoodie. It's nice to see you. Like, all of you." And I wonder what Dad would say if he had been here to see my sort-of first-ever bronze.

The last invitational took about three hours, and this one is on pace for at least that. With some events having over a dozen heats, we all do a lot of sitting around. I'm not in the right mood to circle up with the other kids and break Mr. Tippin's nons to bits today, but that seems to be the Junior Surge standard.

Orion's been living in my head all day and I can't seem to shake him. His leaping plan is more confusing to me than subtracting fractions. And with March just a few days away, we're running out of time. But then I think about his name on that desk. And the letter. And the fight. There's a seedling of doubt in me that I can't ignore. It makes my brain do backflips when I think about how Orion always knows things early. He knew about Mom's home photo studio for newborns. And the Seattle trip. He even knew that I'd eat breakfast with Rhett after joining the swim team. Mom would say that he's an enigma, and she'd surely be right.

Plot idea: *Boy breaks rubix cube to piece it back together correctly.*

My last two events are back-to-back. My 200 freestyle is my favorite event, and I know from the moment I connect with the water that I'm going to be competitive. My breathing is solid. My arms feel strong. My legs don't turn to noodles in the first lap like they usually do. And, when my hands touch the edge, I look up to Rhett kneeling by the block.

"Fourth, dude! Not bad!"

It's a new personal best for me, but I already miss the feeling of a top-three finish.

The relay goes about as well as last time. Patrick and Daniel are the strong links, and Liam and I are the weak ones, especially having just raced solo. Coach Robbins says we're immature to view it that way. "The team is as strong as the team is. No finger pointin'," he always says with a point of his finger. We take second-to-last. Again.

As families and drippy kids mosey toward the doors, I go to grab my gear from the locker room. My plan is to check Room 325. My body is begging me for rest, but I'd like to see Orion today. I don't even care if we just play Battleship or re-sort his trading cards by color again.

"Fritzy, are you in here?" a voice calls from the locker room stairs. It's Rhett.

"Hi?" I answer.

Rhett and Patrick run up the stairs and right up to me as I'm tying my shoes. Rhett is holding a piece of paper in one hand and Patrick has a real impish grin on his face.

"I've peer-edited your writing like a bajillion times at school," Rhett says. "I *know* you can't write in cursive."

"I never learned. Why?"

"Found this in my bag," and he shoves the paper in my face. It's a struggle for me to make sense of scrawly black cursive, but the flowers and hearts scribbled in the margins make an alarm go off in my brain.

Rhett Robbins,

I have to tell you how I feel. I have had a crush on you since the moment I saw your beautiful red hair. Every night I dream of you and how much I want to kiss you. You have made me the happiest boy in Cortland. I am going to swim my hardest for you today!

Your secret admirer,

Christopher Isaac Fritz

p.s. You are the cutest boy in the fifth grade.

p.s.s. Don't show this to anybody else!!!!!!

Plot idea: *Boy stumbles upon his own suicide note that he didn't write.*

"Rhett, this wasn't me. I swear!" My blood runs hot though me. I want to tear the paper up and devour it. Or throw it in the pool. Or scratch everything out with Rhett's marker and run away and hide in a forest for the rest of my life. "Honest. I didn't write this."

"We know," Patrick says with his arms crossed.

"But I think I know who did," Rhett says.

And so do I. Besides Mom and Oakley, there's only one person in all of Cortland who knows my middle name.

CHAPTER 26

Factory Reset

"YOU'VE BEEN GETTING DISTRACTED, Christopher Fritz. Rhett's getting in the way of our progress. I had to do it." Orion talks so casually as he flips through his red journal of photos. Each picture gets a long moment of his attention. He sits crisscross on the edge of the library roof, cars turning in and out below us.

"So your plan was to make him stop talking to me? By making him think I have a crush on him?"

"Pretty much," he says. He's acting like I've just asked him if grass is green. "That's how you talk about him."

"Well it didn't work. It didn't bother him at all. Rhett's still my friend."

"Rhett's a feckless little brat," Orion says as he snaps his book shut. "He needs to learn when to keep his mouth shut."

"Is that why you broke his arm?" Somewhere in the world, ink is spilled on a rug.

Orion's wild horses flash in his eyes. I had planned on being more subtle than that when I practiced confronting imaginary Orion, but here we are. Those practice talks never seem to go as scripted.

"Christopher Fritz. I told you not to believe Rhett Robbins. He's a liar." My heart hijacks my brain controls. I start spitting out everything that's been swirling in the cauldron of my head for the last few days. Finding Orion's desk in Mrs. Correy's room. The fight. His suspension. His claim to be a homeschool kid and the letter I found in his backpack. Orion is passing his journal back and forth in his hands as I spill it all out.

"You have to understand," he says softly. "Everything I have done has been for my father's research."

"How the heck is stomping the snot out of Rhett going to help the research, Orion? That's crap!" Orion puts his head in his hands and squeezes and my heart empties out something it's been hiding away for weeks: "I'm starting to wonder if this whole time travel thing is crap, too."

"We're running out of time." Orion's face tenses up and I can see tears rising in his eyes.

"How are we running out of time? You said your aunt can't find our research if we use Room 325." One of his tears runs loose. Then another. "And this whole leaping thing makes no sense to me. You still haven't told me how it all works. I've been here since January, and I still haven't even met your dad, Orion!"

"Don't speak about my father, Christopher Fritz." His

voice is low. Cold. Direct. "You have no place."

"Excuse me?"

"You won't even talk to your father when you have the chance," he says. "You practically brag about it. And I bet he really wants to talk to you." He stands up and paces along the ledge. A new kind of storm is brewing in his voice. "And it kind of hurts my feelings when you act like that."

"I never know how you're going to *feel* about anything, Orion." He's become skittish. He copies my every step, maintaining a large gap between us. "Sometimes you're happy and fun, and other times you throw things and hit things and scream. I don't always know which Orion I'm going to see every day. And now you're trying to ruin things with Rhett." Orion lowers his head and wipes his eyes. "And I don't know if I can keep doing this with you."

Mom says that words are like toothpaste. Easy to dispense, impossible to put back. And that's why we have to be careful with how we use them. And boy do I wish I could take those ones back.

Orion has dropped his photo journal and become perfectly still. He's a statue crowning the top of the Cortland Community Library. The wind flits his hair and golden scarf in unison. He's otherwise motionless, from the tear trail on his cheek down to his silver, strappy shoes. When he opens his eyes, I look for the wild horses. But they're gone. No waves. No motion. No anger or yelling. I wonder if I've triggered a total factory reset of Orion McBride.

Plot idea: *Boys discovers panacea, destroys it for his own amusement.*

"Orion?" He lets me approach and I put his red book back into his hands. I apologize for what I said and invite him to climb down to play Battleship or Egyptian Rat Killer. Or to go play with Oakley or to go look for his star. Anything. But he doesn't move. His eyes have gone dry. His gaze stings me in a way that reaches way down. I'd rather get a paper cut on my eye than see this look.

"You're a mushroom," he finally says, burying his hands in the pockets of his earthy green shorts. "You're just like Ava Mayfield."

"What?"

"We're done, Chris." He slings on his backpack and begins the climb down.

I grab hold of his backpack and pull him towards me. "Orion, wait. I didn't mean it."

"Yes, you did," he says, freeing himself. He stands on the edge of the climbing ledge. "I can't afford to waste any more time. I'll finish the missions by myself." He turns around and cuts me with his eyes again. "Chris, I hope you never outgrow that hoodie." Then Orion, in an earthy green blur, disappears.

And so does my flame.

CHAPTER 27

Three Lies

I FAKED SICK AGAIN THIS MORNING. I TOLD MOM I still didn't feel good enough to go to swimming practice. But my lie was to Mom's benefit. She was out the door early in a camera-wielding swirl of maple syrup and disorganization. So it's me making sure that Oakley eats breakfast. It's me making sure that she gets dressed for the weather. It's me making sure that the door locks behind me. Two tugs. All secure.

Oakley bounds ahead. "I've got to go! Me and Kadence have a plan today!" she says, barely putting verbal spaces between her words. She dashes off ahead of me, a mad sprint for Weston Elementary.

"Whatever," I say, waving her away. But she's already out of earshot. She bolts onward. The swerve and bounce of her backpack grows smaller and smaller. "I didn't want to walk with you anyway," I lie.

I count my steps as I march to the morning music of echoey birds and tires crushing pavement. Air and earth. Light and heavy. Oakley's all but out of sight now.

Twenty-five steps gone. I tuck my thumbs.

Oakley sure has become a skunk of a little sister, I think as I move. *Impatient. Whiny. Always hurried. But I feel like I miss her. And we live in the same stupid house.*

Fifty steps.

It's Kadence. Kadence has changed my sister. It's like Oakley idolizes her. It's like the curse of her best-friendhood. Or something like that.

Seventy-five.

Best-friendhood. Orion. I kick a rock that whirls into the side of a parked car. "I don't want to think about him," I say into the morning breeze.

One hundred.

Stormy likes that Orion and I are best friends. Or, I guess we were best friends. She always speaks so kindly about him. And everyone. I like that about her. Always seeing the good in people. Even in me.

One hundred twenty-five.

Mr. Tippin doesn't see the good in me. He just sighs at me a lot now. And he always has that disappointed-in-Chris way of talking. Always droning on about grit. Always telling me to take responsibility.

One hundred fifty.

I know what I have to take responsibility for. Dad's accident. And it hurts. I still feel like what happened is my fault.

Way, way down deep. I can feel it. I still want to go back and fix things, but now I think I've lost that chance.

One hundred seventy-five.

I've lost that chance because I lost Orion.

I wrap my arms around my middle and have to remind myself to inhale. I stop at the corner to let a school bus go by ahead of me. I think of Rhett and the swimmers who are probably just now getting out of the water at the middle school.

Two hundred.

I didn't have to confront Orion about that letter. What was I thinking? I had nothing to gain. Rhett was never bothered by it. So why did I do it? Why did I have to go and run my big, miserable, stupid mouth? Why couldn't I just let it go? That's what Dad needed me to do.

Two hundred twenty-five.

I keep hearing it in my head. He didn't even use my full name. He said, "We're done, Chris." And now I think we really are done.

"Hi, Chris!" Ava calls from her circle of friends as I near the playground. Before-school recess. She runs over to me in a hurry to meet me at the fence line.

"Chris, what's wrong?" Ava asks in a whisper. "Why are you crying?"

"I'm fine!" I shove Ava away from me with both hands and head for the doors.

It takes two hundred forty-one steps to get from Willoughby Lane to Weston Elementary School.

CHAPTER 28

Ebb and Flow

MY NOSE HAS ADJUSTED TO THE SMELL OF peanut butter pancakes and eggs. Mom brought dinner in on one of those trays for eating in bed. She even used chocolate chips to turn the top pancake into a goofy smile, the same trick she tried to cheer me up with when I was five. Surely it's all cold by now. I hear mom's slippers shuffling down the hallway. She enters with a smile that has a two-second lifespan. "Critter, please eat."

"I'm not hungry."

"I'm worried about you." She sits on the edge of my bed and checks my forehead with the back of her hand. We both know there is no fever. "How can I help you, Chris? You look so lost right now." She runs one hand through my hair like she used to do. Gentle and smooth. I'll never admit out loud that I love that. Her tablet buzzes on my bed.

"I just need some think time," I say.

"Your teacher called me today."

"Yeah. He said he was going to."

Plot idea: *Boy masters his mind and body, can fall asleep on command.*

"He said that you were hiding in the bathroom for the first two hours of the school day. He thought you were absent." I bunch up my covers and face away from her. "Is something wrong at school? Is someone bullying you?"

"No, Mom." She continues on about how Coach Robbins is also worried because I haven't been to swim practice once this week. I played sick each morning when Rhett came over. But he sees me at school still. He knows I'm fine, but he's too polite with grown-ups to pester.

"Things are just hard right now, Mom," I say with an accidental quiver that I hope she didn't hear. Mom rubs my back gently and it makes my brain go way back. All the way to Oregon. All the way to the days before I was in kinder-garten and Oakley was still crawling. I miss the way Mom used to piggyback me around the house. And the way we'd cuddle when I came into her and Dad's room after bedtime. It used to drive Dad silly, but Mom always let me up. "I just wish we could go back and try things over," I say.

"I do, too," Mom turns off my light and picks up my untouched dishes. I count the steps as she takes them to the kitchen, but she's soon with me again. She sits on the edge of the bed and holds my outstretched hand. "What do you want to do this weekend? I'm ahead of schedule at work and I have some extra time. What should we do?"

"I have my stupid invitational on Saturday. It's all the way in Kennedy," I say into my pillow.

"I say we skip this one," Mom whispers. "I think you and Oakley and I should do something this weekend." I shrug. "Maybe we can see if your friend Orion can come." Somewhere in the world, a child suffers his first bee sting.

"We're not friends anymore," I say.

"Oh no, Critter. What happened?"

"He's just, umm. I don't know." There are more ways to finish that sentence than there are weeks in a year. He's untruthful. He's violent. He's manipulative. But I don't say any of those. "Orion's just kind of a baby."

Plot idea: *Boy pins down the beast, cannot make himself deliver the killing blow.*

Mom says she would normally tell me that friends come and go. That our connections will ebb and flow as we grow up. And it doesn't feel good, but it's normal. "But this feels different," she says thoughtfully. "I like what he brings out in you. I think your pal Orion might be one worth fighting for, Critter. Just think about it."

"Maybe," I say.

"Take off your hoodie. It needs washing."

I do so. As Mom hums down the hallway, I tuck my thumbs and close my eyes.

Hi, Dad. I wish you were here. I'm trying to be strong, but I mucked everything up like I always do. I always make the wrong decisions. And now Orion's upset with me and it feels like someone has shot me full of holes. Mom's so busy lately.

And I have so many things I wish I could talk to you about. Honesty. Friends. Orion. Rhett. God's been fielding most of my questions, assuming he has the time. Or even cares.

I think Mom might be right, too. I think Orion is worth fighting for because I need his help to get you back. But I don't know if Orion wants to fight for me anymore. I'm sorry about all this, Dad. I'm doing my best, but I just feel so heavy. I'll see you soon, hopefully. Transmit back.

CHAPTER 29

Roadkill

My worthless brain still reminds me that Orion has hockey practice on Thursdays. It's a useless reminder at this point. I still look for him in his yard as I pass by after school, but he hasn't been there for a while now. Makes my brain go tumbling, thinking about all the things I would say to him if he was there. Truth is, I miss that kid. A lot. And I want to tell him that.

March has brought emergent color and vibrancy to the formerly lifeless Willoughby Lane. There must be a family of rabbits living around Orion's house because there's a pair of bunnies hiding under Orion's front steps. But there's nobody sitting on top of the steps. And no Arizona plates in the driveway. Actually, the plates have been gone for several days, too. "Did Orion leap back already?" I ask myself, surveying his house for signs of human life. "Did Orion go back without me?"

"Daily!" Stormy cheers when I enter the library. "Shorts? No hoodie? I hardly recognize you!"

"My Mom hid my hoodie because I wore it too much."

"Well you look great in purple, my friend. Glad you're here."

There are no books that need reshelving, because Stormy is too efficient at her job. I don't even look at the Book of the Day's title until I hand it to Stormy. It's called *My Almighty Brain*. Sure would be nice to have one of those.

I take it straight to the tree loft—a sacred reading spot that is almost always overflowing with toddlers and alphabet books—and I open to the first chapter.

Mr. Tippin says he doubts how much I read, which gets my blood going real quick. There's something about low expectations that is more painful than convenient. But I want to prove him wrong. *Success is a job fully done.* Fine then.

Used to be I could get through a book in two days. But ever since Orion ghosted me, I almost always get through the Book of the Day in one sitting. What Mr. Tippin doesn't understand is that I have three hours at the library before Mom picks me up and three hours at home before bed. Plenty of time. It's not like Willoughby Lane is teeming with opportunity and kids to cause mischief with. Not without Orion. And it's not like I can tolerate existing on Earth for more than ten minutes at a time anyway. Stormy's Book of the Day is all I have to look forward to anymore.

I don't think I've ever heard the phone ring in the library before. Stormy answers it after two rings. "Cortland Community Children's Library. Hello! Yes. Yes, Chris is here." I peek from my canopy when I hear my name. I meet Stormy's eyes. "Chris, your mother is on the phone. She wants to talk to you." I'm equal parts annoyed at having to surrender the most revered reading spot in the library and confused as to why Mom is calling me. I wonder if she is going to tell me that she has to stay until midnight or something. Or she got fired. Or she's decided to move back to Oregon and leave me behind. Safe bets all around.

"Hi, Mom?" I say, more a question than a greeting.

"Critter, hi. I need you to walk over to Orion's house right now." My muscles tense up real tight.

"Why?"

"I've already talked with Lillian McBride. Please, go. I'll be there as soon as I can."

Plot idea: *Mom coaxes boy over crocodile pit with cotton candy.*

"Oh, and Chris," I hear Mom say before I hand the phone back.

"Yeah?"

"I need you to be a grownup for today. Be strong. I'll be there soon," she says before hanging up. I shrug at Stormy and take my time collecting my things.

I can feel water sloshing around in my stomach as I reach Willoughby Lane. I want to see Orion. But something feels off. If Mom is trying to intervene so Orion and I will talk, then she clearly doesn't know Orion. Once he gets his brain on something, that's it. He's got a resolve that would make Coach Robbins beam.

Arizona plates are now here.

Mom's lucky that I don't have a house key yet. Every cell I have wants to make a run for my own front door. But the thought of seeing Orion pulls me. It makes me want to cry. He'd call me a *heart boy* if he knew that.

Four knocks. The door opens and I say a silent prayer to God to show me mercy today. Orion McBride's archnemesis towers over me like a vulture over roadkill. "Chris, hello. My name is Lillian McBride. Please come in."

CHAPTER 30

The Little Lark

"CHRIS, LET ME GET YOU SOME WATER. GO ahead and have a seat." I forgot how colorless and motionless Orion's house is. The last time I was in here was the first day I met him. That day is tucked in my brain's memory files under *road rash* and *breaking apart my understanding of the universe.* I wonder if Orion's bedroom is still the same coloring book stronghold it was before.

Lillian sets down two glasses of water. She chugs hers down quickly, almost tempting me to do the same. But I've read enough stories to know what this is. I'm not getting poisoned today. At least not this easily. It still makes me uneasy how *normal* Lillian looks. All her buttoned-up tallness and soft speaking voice. It's a ruse if I've ever seen one.

"Chris, thank you again for coming over. It's very important."

"What's going on?" I ask, trying to show mistrust in my voice.

"Please be patient with me. I'm still relearning how to talk to children. Orion says I speak an ancient language." She has the same crispness to her words that Mr. Tippin has. My guess would be that whatever she does for a job, it involves lots of talking. That, or she's as loony as Orion and she talks to herself all day. "If you have questions, please do ask. Okay?"

"Alright," I say. I want to give her as few words as possible.

"Chris, what do you know about this?" And from a handbag resting over her chair she pulls out Orion's red photo journal. She places it on the table between us, strap fastened. My soul glitches out when I see it. Orion said that our first leaping attempt was ruined because Lillian found the research and sabotaged it. I tuck my thumbs. Orion needs to know that I am not giving her a single word.

"I've never seen that before," I say.

"Really? Because you're on almost every page." Lillian unstraps the cover and slowly turns through the pictures for me to see. Memories flood back to me like fireflies lighting up a clearing. There we are on the roof for our first ever mission picture. And there's the hot chocolate from Mrs. Howard. And the day we tried on Andre's costumes. Oakley. Kadence. Me. Me. The day we drew portraits. The day we tried to catch a squirrel. His annihilated green bike. There's even one of me from the Cortland Invitational. I'm diving in, frozen in the air with Liam looking up at me from the water. That must've been during my relay. That must've been when Orion planted that letter to Rhett. "Seems like you might be remembering," Lillian says.

"A little," I lie.

"I know what this is," she says, shutting the journal and resetting the strap. "I have a very important favor to ask of you, Chris. And it's why I asked you to come over today." I know what she's going to say. I'm ready for it. My brain and heart are in tandem—for once—and are ready to defend Orion. I have all my words lined up and ready to fire. Leaping back to Dad is too important to give it all up now. I tighten my jaw. "Chris," she says, "I want you to fill this journal completely with photos."

Plot idea: *Boy goes all-in with seven high against the Devil, the Devil folds.*

"Excuse me?" I ask. She repeats her instructions. She says that she wants us to go on more adventures because *that sweet Orion needs it.* I can tell she's fighting back tears. I'm becoming too familiar with that face. "Is he here? Upstairs?"

"No, he's out right now. You and I are going to get him in a little while."

"Right," I say. "It's Thursday. Hockey day."

Lillian slaps the table and lets out a mighty, singular laugh. "Hockey? Is that what the little lark told you?" I can see from her smile that she's picturing Orion on ice skates. I hope Orion doesn't get that part of my transmission, because it is a little bit funny to me, too. Lillian says that she'd love for Orion to play hockey so he can improve his "*gross motor functioning*," which does sound like something a villain might say. "On Thursdays, Orion spends an hour with his counselor."

"His *counselor*? Why does Orion go to a counselor?" Lillian gives me a long, long look like she's waiting for me to remember something. Like she's waiting to see if I'm just playing dumb. She relents.

"Chris, there are things you need to know about Orion. And he's going to be *very* upset with me when he finds out about this conversation. I'm going to take a wild guess and say that Orion's been making things up for you," she says. Somewhere in the world, an archer hits the bullseye. "But I want you to know what's going on with our sweet boy."

The most masterful pretender in the history of kids, I think. Nothing at this table has gone the way I expected it to so far. But I wonder if this is what Orion expected, which is why he didn't want me to meet Lillian in the first place. Orion would have me put to the sword for this, but I choose to trust Lillian.

"Okay," I say.

"Do you know what *grief* is, Chris?"

"Kind of," I say, selling short many characters I've met in stories.

"Grief is a heavy, heavy feeling. It's an incredible sorrow that one feels alongside loss."

"Right."

"Orion is carrying an unbelievable amount of grief. And he doesn't always know what to do with it or how to ask for help. He's in denial, which is a perfectly normal part of this process."

"I don't understand," I say. My brain sifts through all of our leaping research for clues. "What's he denying?"

Lillian shuts her eyes. "Orion's father is very sick, Chris. He has been sick for a while now." My heartbeat slows down, and the room temperature drops.

"What?" I ask. Electricity flashes inside me.

"Last summer, we learned that his father, Matthias, probably had about twelve months left. I came here to care for my ailing brother, and help his loving, grief-stricken son.

"From Arizona," I say. Lillian nods. My brain goes all the way back to Orion's explanation. Everything got bad when Lillian moved in.

"Today, things are progressing awfully quickly," she explains. "The original twelve months would be a bit of a miracle at this point." Somewhere in the world, a river runs dry, its last drop fighting, fighting, trickling away. "Just before Christmas, we received some dire news from our doctors about Matthias's progress. Orion lashed out at school the next day and earned himself a hearty suspension."

"The kids still talk about that," I say. Lillian looks unsurprised.

"That poor boy he hurt," Lillian says as she folds her hands as though in prayer. "Orion did *monstrous* damage that day." I can see on her face that she knows the same

Orion who fell off his bike. An Orion overtaken by rage. Or perhaps not simply rage. Perhaps fear. Perhaps grief.

"We decided during his suspension that having time now with his father is what mattered most. So, we pulled him out of school for the time being."

"He's not still suspended? All the kids think that's why he's gone."

"His suspension was for eight days, which was probably more grace than he deserved. We simply knew that Orion wouldn't be able to focus on his learning with the war going on his heart." I tell Lillian that it makes a lot of sense. That sometimes Orion can heat up or grow distant with seemingly no warning. "That boy likes to think he leads with his head the way his father does," she says. "But Orion leads with his beautiful, expressive, wild heart. And we love that about him." Somewhere in the world, Orion just spontaneously combusted. "It's such a joy to see the way Orion plays with and talks to his father, even now."

"Is Mr. McBride here? I've never met him."

"No, sweetie. He's been in intensive care for weeks. Orion spends time with him most mornings. When Matthias has any amount of stamina, Orion is the one he wants to be with."

"But your car is almost never here," I say. "Does Orion live here alone?"

"No, Chris," she laughs. "Though I love your confidence in him. Orion moved in with me last November. I'm renting an apartment up past Madison Park."

"What!" I burst. "He's here every day after school!" I wonder for a second if we are talking about the same Orion McBride. Surely there aren't two kids with that name in this town who have aunts from Arizona and red photo journals. Surely there is hope for my dimming, whispering flame. "I'm kind of confused, I'm sorry."

"I understand, Chris. If Orion hasn't been straight with you, I'm sure this is a lot to take in." Lillian McBride just set a new world record for the greatest understatement of all time. "Orion lives with me. Most mornings, he spends some time with his father at Cortland Memorial Hospital. That is, if Matthias can."

"Yeah, I get that," I say.

"After our visit, we usually grab lunch and try to do *some* schoolwork activities. Nadine Correy from the school provides us with resources. That can be hit and miss on our end." My brain goes back to the letter from Orion's backpack. That he's *always welcome to come visit.* I shake my head, wondering when exactly I became the densest boy in the history of boys.

"It's so hard on Orion to see Matthias in his current condition. He needs time to rest his poor heart." I take a sip of the water that's been waiting. "I bring him back to his house here so that he can have some alone time."

"So, he just hangs out here by himself?" I ask.

"He needs the reprieve," she says. Lillian explains that as soon as they leave the hospital after a visit, Orion's clouds roll in and he changes. He'll veer in and out of denial, often refusing to talk about the situation. She says that he's still learning how to communicate his feelings and thoughts in healthy ways. "He tries to keep it all locked up," she says. "And sometimes that causes meltdowns of different sorts."

"I think I've seen that before," I say.

"He needs time to process his world in a place that's comfortable. He feeds his fish and plays on his computer for a while. But do you know the main reason he kept coming all winter? The reason he'd beg to return here to Willoughby Lane almost every day?

"What?"

"A boy named Christopher Fritz."

"Me?" I ask. Lillian smiles. "You've known about me?" She can see the confusion on my face. I thought I had been a secret this whole time.

"If this red photo book is new to you, then you have no idea how much joy and light you've given Orion and Matthias. You've been a real friend to him."

I drop the act. "I've just been following Orion's lead with all those pictures," I say. "I haven't done anything." Lillian looks off. I can't see what she is picturing, but the dining room lights dance in her shimmering eyes. She clears her throat and holds her empty glass with two hands.

"Matthias worries that he's stealing away Orion's childhood."

"What does that mean?" I ask.

"It means that Orion is doing so much worrying. So much hurting. He's not getting to just be a boy. So Matthias writes him a goal whenever he can. It's so sweet, they call them *missions*." Air escapes my lungs and cannot get back in. "They're small things. Things that can help Orion get back the time he's lost to grief."

"Get back the time," I repeat. I cross my arms. Tight.

Watch a sunset.

Find something worth keeping.

Make some music.

"He'll rush to Matthias with his finished card and photo in hand, dizzy with excitement. He'll retell every detail and the two of them will laugh and talk and dream and laugh." It's like she's seeing it all play out right here at the table. "You may not know it, Chris, but because of your adventures in this book," she passes the photo journal to me, "Matthias gets to see his little boy be a little boy again. It's almost like stepping back in time."

I hold myself tight. Tight enough to split in two. Or ten. My flame is out. Drowned by all the tears I've been trying to lock away. But they find daylight. And I wail.

Lillian asks if I'm okay, and I do exactly what Orion would expect me to do. My heart takes over and I let everything out. I tell her about the mission cards. I tell her about how we were supposed to go back in time. I tell her about being *the kid of the killer*, and the Mariners, and how Orion's plan was my only way back to Oregon. To my dream of being an author. To Dad.

"Sweet, child," Lillian says. My eyes burn deep, deep, deep. I rest my forehead on the tabletop. "This hurts you, too. I hear you. And I'm sorry that Orion's denial led you to this."

"I get why he did it," I say. My words are hardly audible to even me. "He's fighting hard."

"And that is truly why I've asked you to come over today, Chris," she says. I shut my eyes. "Orion won't open up about what happened between you two, but I know you're not talking. And he needs you, Chris. And I think you need him, too." I am grateful that I have no more tears to lose. "Things are likely to get worse before they get better."

"What do you mean?" I ask, afraid I already know.

"Our wonderful doctors are doing everything they can do. And there is always room for a miracle." Her words carry no belief in that. "But Orion is going to need a friend very soon. His destructive behavior has cost him a lot of friends. And when I look through these pictures, I see that you've given Orion a light that he's been missing for a long while."

Plot idea: *The window is actually a mirror; boy comprehends his own reflection for the first time.*

"Chris, you are your own person. You have to make your own decisions. I simply want to ask that you look in your heart to give Orion another chance. Please fill this book up with adventures and stories and memories. Orion needs it more than any of us could ever understand."

"Can I ask a question?" I say, trying to not sound shy.

"Anything."

I trip over my words several times because I'm worried about sounding rude. But then I spit it out bluntly and hope for the best. "What'll happen to Orion if his dad passes away?"

Lillian nods slowly and says, "I will adopt him."

CHAPTER 31

The Executive Director

"WHAT?!" MY CHAIR FALLS BACK AS I burst through the ceiling and into the atmosphere. "He's moving to Arizona?" Turns out I did have more tears in reserve. "Orion can't go!"

"Chris."

"He can't leave! He's the only thing I have! He's the only good thing about Willoughby Lane! And Cortland! Not having him lately has been needles in my eyes." I pace aimlessly into the empty living room, both thumbs tucked tighter than ever. "I miss him. I need him *here*." I line the words up just right in my brain. "Please don't take Orion away."

"Chris, it's going to be fine. Orion isn't going anywhere."

Somewhere in the world, fireworks launch.

I'm somewhere between crying and laughing as I silently thank God for hearing me on that one. "Matthias is firm on this. He wants Orion here, and I've come to agree that this is the best place for him. He'll be moving off of Willoughby Lane, but we're staying in town." I exhale the sweetest tasting breath in the history of me.

"And he'll come to middle school next year?" I wonder about how his unsteady hands would fare in a game of dodgeball, or he if could ever work a violin. He'd probably struggle with a locker.

"Orion will be repeating fifth grade at a different elementary school. He's missed far too much school to move on, and we think he'd benefit from having a new start with new peers."

"Darn," I say. "That makes sense." Mom says that sometimes we have to zoom out to see a bigger picture. Orion staying here is as far out as I can zoom. As long as he is here I couldn't care less where he goes to school. It's probably for his own good that he gets out of Weston at this point.

"He's too much a part of the community fabric to move him now," Lillian says. "He has so many valuable connections because of the work Matthias has done here."

"As a scientist?" I ask. Lillian rolls her eyes as she mouths a word I would get in trouble for saying.

"Matthias served as the executive director of the Cortland Community Library for over twenty years."

"Are you serious?" I ask. I wonder for a moment how

much Orion *has* been honest about. If it wasn't for this conversation, I'd question if his name is actually Orion.

"Matthias loved two things: Cortland and stories. He made such a fuss after reading, oh, what was it?" My brain already has a pretty good guess. "Oh! *The Little Prince.*"

Of course.

She tells me that Matthias was so infatuated by *The Little Prince* that he proposed a large-scale expansion of the children's section and funded it in under a year. "What used to be just a few novice texts on some low shelves in the corner became its own beautiful half of the building.

"It's pretty great. I've spent a lot of time in there this year," I say. That makes Lillian smile again.

"Oh, Chris, but there's more. The story of *The Little Prince* lingered in his head for years. He called me one Sunday and said that he was going to do something crazy. Something neither of us thought we'd ever do: He was going to adopt a child."

"And that child was...?"

"Orion," she says. "Age three." I wonder if Orion had ever mentioned his adoption when I wasn't paying attention. It never occurred to me that he may have been adopted. But I can hear Mom saying that it's not even a question worth asking. "And those two tamed each other *instantly*," she says.

"Tamed?" I ask.

"Oh, it was so sweet." Nostalgia swirls in her voice. "Matthias re-purposed one of the open offices upstairs into a playroom so he could take Orion to work with him. Orion grew up in that library. I bet he knows more about it than the current employees."

Plot idea: *Boy solves the lost cipher, the answers to all the world's questions lie before him.*

"Thanks for telling me all of this. There was a lot I didn't know," I say.

"Thank you for coming, Chris. No matter what happens, I hope Orion has many more adventures with you."

"I do, too," I say.

"You've done a lot to help him process his world. Orion has to accept his pain in order to heal from it."

And nothing in the history of the world has ever made more sense.

CHAPTER 32

Artwork

I T'S BEEN STUCK IN MY HEAD FOR A FEW DAYS now. The large blue sign of *Mountainview Counseling Services, LLC.* The sight of Orion's moppy hair through the office window. The way he screamed, *"You weren't supposed to tell!"* when he saw me in the car with Lillian. All of Cortland heard that. The way he sprinted through traffic and hopped a fence into someone's backyard. I offered to go after him. I told Lillian that I'm a swimmer and I have a lot of stamina. But she shook her head and told me that Orion knows the way home. That it wasn't the first time.

That was Thursday.

It's been three days and I still haven't seen him. I check his front steps regularly, and I've even made a few trips over to Room 325 just to see. I want to run loose with him. With spring slowly tearing winter apart each day, I can hear the roads and sidewalks whispering. Begging us to zig and to zag with a camera in hand and a mission in focus. But I still worry our mission days are done.

My brain does all sorts of twists and turns because of what Lillian said. *Orion has to accept his pain in order to heal from it.*

I've never understood him as much as I do now. Everything we've done has been a hideaway for him. If he denies the truth, there's nothing to heal from. And if he can't heal his bleeding heart, his wild horses run free. The tempest. The storytelling. Mom says that I shouldn't associate with people who can't tell the truth, but I don't think this is regular schoolyard dishonesty. I think it's survival.

But I need to take my mind off of it. And there's one person I know who's always good for a distraction.

"Hi, Oakley," I say. She's making her bed, carefully arranging the giraffe and the hippo. Stardust, now earless, still sits front and center. Makes my eyes twitch to remember how that toy's injury happened.

"What do you want?" she asks. She doesn't even turn around to look at me.

"Want to make a book?" I ask. And Oakley almost knocks me over as she races out with her pencil box in hand.

Oakley and I work on the kitchen table. As usual, she hogs all the good markers. But I let her. Just for today. Back in Oregon, we used to work on the same story together. I'd write, she'd illustrate. But today, we both have our own projects in mind. Oakley is creating her own fantasy story about two kitten spies trying to recover the lost jewels of an island nation. Still untitled. "I always thought of Kadence as a piglet, not a cat," I say. Oakley dashes my arm with a green marker.

I try to ignore Mom as she sneaks pictures from the living room with her phone. I focus on my story, *The Little Lark*. The tale of a small, silver bird who travels to the sun to bring wing-loads of sunlight and warmth back to a city stuck in a frigid twilight. I'm no good at drawing birds, but at least the sun is easy. I'm thankful for a phone call that renders Mom's camera unusable. I trade Oakley for a yellow.

"Good morning, Lillian," Mom says from the living room couch. "Yes, he's here." I turn. "No. No. Let me ask." Mom covers the phone receiver with one hand. "Critter, have you seen Orion today?"

"No. I checked like an hour ago, but he wasn't home." Mom returns to the phone. Her urgent voice has halted all drawing. Oakley and I trade uncertain gazes.

"Chris, are you telling the truth?" Mom asks.

"Yes. I haven't seen him since Thursday."

"Orion's missing and there's an emergency. He needs to be at the hospital."

Somewhere in the sky, a star flickers for life.

PART 3

The Storytellers

CHAPTER 33

Wildland

ORION WILL GO NUCLEAR WHEN HE FINDS OUT that I spilled the beans about Room 325. But I heard it in Mom's voice. The way she said *emergency*. It was painfully familiar. I've never asked for more crimson-red zoom from my trusty three-speeder.

I rip around the corner and toss my bike to the ground, but my eyes see it right away. I won't be climbing to Room 325 anymore. The thin branch we used to climb up from the air conditioning unit lies pathetically on the ground. Looks like Orion gave it the old Rhett Robbins treatment. What's more is that our window isn't propped open like normal. My only way in is dead shut. "But he had to be in there to shut it," I say to myself. And if he's there, he's certainly no dummy. The door is definitely locked.

"Woah, kiddo!" a teenager says from Stormy's chair. She doesn't work on Sundays. "Walking feet only please!"

"I need the key to Room 325. It's an emergency."

"Excuse me?"

"There's someone locked in Room 325. In the old part of the building. I need the key."

"Nobody uses that part of the building, kiddo. I don't even have those keys. And you're only, like, the third person in today." I want to scream and go blast the door down myself. But then I remember what Lillian said about Orion's early days. He grew up here. He knows the place better than anybody.

And something inside me lights.

How lucky it was for Orion to bring his green football that day we found the room. Even more lucky that he stood in just the right spot and threw the ball just wildly enough. And how *unbelievably lucky* that the ball went tumbling through the only open window on an unused section of the building. "What a lucky little storyteller," I whisper to God.

I set the world record for fastest bike ride ever from the Cortland Community Library to Willoughby Lane and nearly cause Orion's house more bike damage as I struggle to stop. Kitchen door unlocked. I take what I came for from his bedroom and set the world record again on my way back to the library.

Our room is easy to find from this side. There aren't many rooms upstairs anyway, and only one of them is labeled with any numbers at all.

A small silver key on a black string fits the locked door of Room 325 perfectly.

Plot idea: *Junior sleuth solves the case with the lint in his own pocket.*

The door to Room 325—Orion's former playroom—opens soundlessly. Caught in an ocean of scattered papers, pictures, and books is Orion McBride. Black shorts. He's on all fours with a copy of *The Little Prince* pinned to the floor. We make exactly one millisecond of eye contact. He's back in his book.

"Orion, people are looking for you. We have to go." I grab his arm, but he swats at me.

"I'm literally not leaving until I find what I need," he says. "I've read this book seventy-four times now and I'm not going to fail. I'm close. The invisible. The *essential*. I need to find my answer."

"Orion, stop. Your aunt called. They need you at the hospital. It's an emergency."

"It's always an emergency," he says. His voice is low. Clear. Wounded. "It was an emergency this morning, too." He sits back on his feet. "And he looked so bad, Christopher Fritz. It was so bad." Whatever Orion is seeing, it's twisting his face up. "There has to be something I can do. My father always says that all the answers I need are in this book, and I *have* to find them. Now."

I crouch down and try to close his book, but when Orion's heart is determined, he's metal. He turns away from me.

"I don't think this book is going to help you. Leaving with me right now will help you. Let's go!" Orion pauses.

Wild horses rear their heads in his eyes.

"I need to do something," he says. His hands quicken, nearly tearing each page he turns. "I don't want to see him hurt anymore, Christopher Fritz," he says, swiping tears from his cheeks. "I've read so much. I've read website after article after medical journal after medicine bottle, hoping to find something to help the doctors see what they've missed."

"Orion," I try to interrupt.

"I've studied everything I could. I did every mission he told me to do. I read this stupid book over and over and over again. And nothing's working, Christopher Fritz!" He punches himself in the head. I reach for his hands, but he pushes me down to the floor. He's losing control. Words become screams. Gold fades to black. "All my leads just fall off a cliff. And I feel like *I'm* falling off a cliff right now!"

"Let me help, Orion," I plead.

"I don't want to be scared anymore. I don't want to cry anymore." He wraps himself up in a hug as the tears rush. He drops again to his knees. "I just want to help him. I want to go back. I just want my daddy." He looks like such a small child.

"Then let's go. Please. Let's go see him," I say. I lift Orion to his feet, but he limps over to the large window and rests his head on the glass. He holds his book tight.

"I'm tired of not knowing what's going to happen. Of being scared each night. Of not knowing if he'll be there when I wake up." Horses flee an oncoming tempest. "I'm so tired of reading this worthless book for invisible answers that don't even exist." he shouts as he spikes the book into the floor. "I'm so tired of taking pictures. And being angry." The cracked dam bursts. "And I'm so tired of *feeling like this!*"

Two closed fists slam. Stars explode. Worlds crumble. The entire window explodes into a slow-motion masterpiece. Shards of glass flicker, flash, slash, and then sing as they rain onto the cold floor. Orion falls to his knees, motionless, arms out to the open world before him.

"Orion!" I run to his front. His eyes are sealed. His body quivering. His arms. "Your arms, Orion! Oh my God!" Blood.

Way.

Too.

Much.

Blood.

I scream for help into the hallway with everything I have. Once, twice, five times.

The entire world blurs and I can't find my breath. So much of Orion is dripping out onto the floor. It's a ruby red wildland of glass, research, and, surely, his spirit. He's frozen in place, as if completely lost to time.

Finally.

I'm pushed out of the doorway by Lillian and the teenage employee.

More screaming. More crying. I rest my head on the

ground as my eyes struggle to refocus. Lillian scoops Orion up like an infant and runs.

"I'm sorry," Orion says softly. And I'm not sure if he was talking to me or to Lillian. Or to God. Or maybe even just the window.

Plot revision: *The boy made of sunshine does bleed after all.*

CHAPTER 34

Flash of Yellow

MATTHIAS MCBRIDE PASSED AWAY AT 1:52 on Monday morning.

CHAPTER 35

No Shorts

I'VE NEVER BEEN TO A FUNERAL BEFORE.

I tried to find Orion when we arrived, but Mom held my hand tight. "Critter, let him come to you today." Flowers. Black clothes. Forlorn faces. A slideshow of Matthias McBride cycling slowly on two large screens. Orion's in so many of the pictures: There he is on a bike with training wheels, a selfie from the front seat of a car, a victorious duo with two caught fish. The guests chuckle when they see Orion's disgusted face as he holds up his catch.

And there's one picture from a place that maybe only I will recognize. Orion and his dad are on the roof of the library with a bag of popcorn. Legs dangling. Golden scarf flowing. I miss that smile.

"*I hate that smell!*" he had yelled the first day we went up there. I think I get it now.

Mom and I didn't arrive early enough to get seats. She thought better of bringing Oakley at the last minute and was able to drop her off at Kadence's. I'm grateful for that. I don't like when Oakley sees me cry.

From the back of the church, I can see Ava and several other fifth graders. Mr. Tippin and Mrs. Correy are close to the middle on the right side. I forget that Orion was Mrs. Correy's student. She probably hasn't seen him since he did a number on Rhett.

Stormy's here along with several of the library employees. There's Lillian. I would have expected her to sit in front. Andre. Mrs. Howard. Most all of Cortland, it seems. But I don't see Orion. I'm surprised for a small moment, but then I'm not.

There is a prayer. And a speech. And someone from the library board of directors speaks about how much focus and love Matthias put into energizing the literacy of the community's youth and blah blah blah. Makes me wonder if Orion is going to have to talk. For his sake, I hope not. I catch my attention drifting.

Plot idea: *Boy's brain gets hijacked by two troublesome whispers.*

Whisper number one makes me a skeptic: God scares me sometimes. Life scares me sometimes. I don't think I could ever tell Mom about it. About the doubt that overtakes me now and then and makes me question how closely God is even listening, if at all. To me? To Dad? To Orion? She'd call me a doubting Thomas. But it's hard. It shakes all the foundations that hold me up. I've never had the right words in my brain to talk about it.

Whisper number two makes me a bad person: I'm jealous that Orion's dad gets a farewell ceremony. But I won't admit that out loud.

As the guests filter out into the cool spring morning, I ask Mom if I can say hi to Lillian. She reminds me to be thoughtful with my words. Once I get closer, I see Orion lying down in the pew with his head in Lillian's lap. Eyes shut. The rise and fall of every breath. Dress pants today. No shorts. A tearful Lillian waves hello to me as she runs her fingers through Orion's thick, wild hair. Makes me wonder if he really is tired or if his heart just couldn't do this today. He's discarded his jacket to the floor, and each arm is bandaged up from forearm to wrist. I want to ask Dad about inside scars and outside scars and which ones heal faster.

I let Orion have his sleep.

CHAPTER 36

Corner Pieces

THERE ARE PICTURE BOOKS EVERYWHERE. Dozens. Some spread out, some stacked up. Stormy is explaining to me their many different categories, genres, and reading levels. "If you really want to write picture books, you have to know the nuances of the art form, Daily. You have to know the market." She's arranging them into groups based on what she calls their *readability*. It's contagious when Stormy gets this excited about something. I pick up one book from her *early readers* stack. There is a boy on the cover jetpacking through space, triumphant fist raised high.

"This one reminds me of Orion," I say mostly to myself.

"How's little Booker doing? Have you seen him?"

"No. No yet." I tell her that I'm nervous to see him because I don't know what to say when I do. I'm worried that if I mention his dad, he might fall apart like a sandcastle. But I can't just act like nothing has happened.

By now, every employee here knows that we were stowed away in Room 325 and that Orion's lucky to still have two hands and ten fingers. I'm surprised that I'm still allowed to come inside the building after what we did. I'm more surprised that pretty much nobody was upset when word got out about it. "Sounds like Orion," one employee had said with a jovial shrug.

"So much of what he said was made up," I say, tapping the picture book stacks straight.

"But you can understand why, right?" Stormy asks. "I don't think he meant any harm." I agree with her, saying that I wish Orion could have been more honest with me. Especially about Matthias.

"More honest with you?" Stormy asks. "Daily, how honest have *you* been since you moved here?" Her question catches me by surprise.

"What?" I ask.

"What about when you lied to your mom right here at my desk?" she asks. I shrug, looking at my shoes. "Have you talked with your teacher about how it frustrates you that he doesn't trust you? Or to that swimmer boy about how it hurt your feelings when he made fun of Booker?" Stormy's on a roll. She's not letting me break eye contact. "I love that you tell me things, Daily. But I worry that you've been avoiding hard conversations."

Plot idea: *Boy clad in gold armor undone by all-seeing sorceress.*

I change the subject. "I'm worried about Orion," I say.

Stormy smiles. She knows that that was a checkmate. "He hasn't left his house in four days." Stormy starts the same speech Mom has been giving me about letting him grieve at his own pace. "His aunt says he won't even talk," I say. "I just wish I could help him."

"Daily," Stormy says with softness taking over her voice, "You might be exactly who he needs right now. If any kid in this town can help him, it's probably you."

"But I don't know what to do. I don't know what to say. My words always seem to tear things apart." I retreat to the picture book in front of me.

"If there were magic words that could soothe a grieving heart, surely someone would have already said them by now. He's your best friend."

"But what should I do if he won't even talk to me?"

"Daily, stop," she says. She looks at me directly. "Don't run from this. There's no correct answer or perfect speech to give. If what Booker needs is a friend, then *you* can give that to him." She forces the book shut that I've opened. "Remember that story he's always going on and on about?"

"*The Little Prince*?" I ask.

"Yup. Remember what the fox said to the Little Prince about taming?" I try to stretch my brain way back to remember, but nothing comes to mind. I shake my head no. "You are responsible for what you've tamed," she says. I let those words bounce around in me for a moment.

"Tamed?" I ask. Lillian had used that word, too.

"You two are connected," Stormy says. "And that's what matters most. Taking care of connection isn't just about being kind. It's not for your convenience. It's your responsibility, Daily."

"I'm responsible for what I've tamed," I repeat, the fox's words now ringing deep, deep inside me.

"Forever," Stormy nods.

Plot idea: *After placing 996 pieces of the puzzle, boy finally finds the corner pieces.*

My brain goes way back again to the day Orion came over for music lessons with Oakley. Did he really just come to make music for the mission that day? Or maybe, somehow, he knew I was drifting apart from my sister? I remember it so clearly. He barged into my house and tossed his energy around like leaves without asking for permission to do either. I remember how it felt to watch him play with Oakley and Kadence. And I remember how it felt when I finally joined. It was like warm pajamas straight out of the dryer. And that gives me an idea. I'll take my world to him. And I won't ask for permission.

The maximum number of books one person can check out is thirty. So I check out thirty.

CHAPTER 37

Dot-to-Dot

TWELVE STEEP STAIRS UP TO A LONELY wooden door. Lillian warns me that Orion might not be himself. That he's *doing this at his own pace*. I count down from five with my hand on the doorknob. My brain wants to let him be. But my heart has a responsibility to my best friend. I open the door to the coloring book world Orion has made for himself.

Orion is lying on top of his covers. The little rockets on his pajamas have the same shining red color as the haunting, jagged lines on his unbandaged arms. I wonder how long those glass scars will linger.

When he sees me, he immediately rolls over onto his side away from me. I expected that he would be crying, but he's as silent and still as Willoughby Lane was on the day we met. My brain sparks and teeters in my head as I try to figure out which words to use. I've been rehearsing all day, but seeing Orion now makes all my words turn to jelly. "Hi, Orion," I say. *Better than nothing.* He's silent.

I quietly move around Orion's bed and towards his purple bean bag chair that sits under the lamp and the thud of my backpack hitting the floor startles even me. Lots of books. I expect Orion to roll away from me again when I fall into the bean bag, but he doesn't.

We hold eye contact for a moment, and I can see a flash of confusion on his face when I dump out thirty library books from my backpack onto his floor.

"Orion?" I ask. I'm hopeful for an answer, but all I get is his gaze. "I miss you. A lot. I want to help you if I can, but I'm not really sure how. I know you love stories." He looks at me blankly. All the rain clouds and horses have been drained out of him. "So I brought you some." He shuts his eyes. I pick up *Onwards and Backwards*, the very same book that earned Orion his nickname at the library. I open it up to page one and say the chapter title. And before Orion can protest, I start reading the book out loud. I read proudly and slowly. I look up after every third word. He's staring right at me. He hasn't rolled away or hasn't asked me to leave. So I keep reading.

And I read.

And read.

After fifteen pages, Orion starts to trace the cuts on his arms with his finger.

After twenty-eight pages, I can hear him sniffling into his bed sheets. But I pretend not to notice. I look up often during the first *Booker, Templeton* scene, hoping I might catch a smile. But no. I'll just have to keep on hoping as we go.

Lillian comes up and stands in the doorway. I hadn't heard her climbing the stairs. Orion stays facing me, so I don't think he noticed her either. She waves me on and she smiles real big from the doorway as I read more. She stays like that for a good three chapters before taking her quiet leave.

After sixty-six pages of *Onwards and Backwards* I notice that familiar pattern of long inhale, short exhale. Long, short. He's asleep. "Orion?" I whisper. Out like a baby. I study him from the bean bag chair. I wonder about dreams and if there is any peace where he is right now. He deserves some, that's for sure. I stand up to stretch my legs and hover quietly around Orion's room. His fish tank fills the space with a hum of blue light and soft sound. I peek again to see if maybe he's watching me.

Still out.

I never did get a good look at all the pictures on his bulletin board during my first trip here. Dozens. And many of me now, too. There's that girl with the backwards hat in a lot of the photos. And now I know who she is: Ava Mayfield. Some of the pictures were taken right here in this room, some at school. "Ava's tamed him, too," I whisper to myself.

I think of all the questions Ava is always asking about him. How she asked, "*Does he still live on Willoughby*

Lane?" like she knew he would be moving. She's the one who lit Orion's fuse the day he hurt Rhett. And then I see that white and blue polaroid camera sitting underneath the bulletin board. *AM/OM* scrawled fancifully by the lens in black ink. Initials.

Plot idea: *Boy sets world record for longest-ever dot-to-dot completed.*

Those two were friends.

Wait, no.

They *are* friends. The me that first moved to Willoughby Lane would have been jealous to know that Orion had such a rich, well-documented history with another friend. But now it makes me happy to see all of these Ava pictures. It makes me happy that there are other kids in Orion's corner. Worrying about him. Cheering for him. Maybe that's what Stormy was talking about when she said I needed to be an ally and not an obstacle. Maybe.

With Orion still passed out, I leave my backpack and books in his room and ask Lillian if I can come back tomorrow. "Please do," she says.

Tuesday. Oakley comes with me this time. We read some of the new books we're making at home, and Oakley reads her all-time favorite picture book—*My Bashful Monster*—to Orion twice. It's fun to hear how confident and smooth her reading has become since the last time I heard her read out loud. That was back in Oregon. Not even Oakley's goofy character voices can force Orion to crack a smile, but his eyes stay with her the whole time.

Wednesday. I set a sealed letter on Orion's computer keyboard. "Ava Mayfield asked me to bring this to you," I say. "She said it's no hurry." I'm glad to see Orion is wearing different pajamas today. Signs of life. Lillian says he's eating and moving, but only when nobody's watching. I asked if she knows why, but she would only say that *Orion's doing his best right now*.

"We're probably going to finish *Onwards and Backwards* today," I say as I plop into the purple bean bag. "I'm taking requests for new stories." He rolls flat on his back. "Just think about it," I say as I open to my latest folded corner and read the newest chapter title aloud.

I've gotten good at reading a sentence quickly in my head and delivering it slow so I can watch him. Sometimes I pretend to be confused about the story in hopes that he will spring up and want to teach me. But nothing. The last page comes and goes without Orion uttering a single sound.

As I'm browsing the summaries of other books to read, I notice that Orion has fallen asleep again. Up. Down. I pick up *The Little Prince*. This one had seemed like a good idea when I grabbed it at the library, but now I'm not so sure. It makes me think about the day of the emergency. "Maybe another day," I whisper to myself.

I had planned on reading *The Little Prince* a second time for myself, but I never quite got around to it. I had wanted to *seek to understand*, as Stormy had said. With Orion out like a light, now is as good a time as any. I open the story.

This time, I'm prepared for the odd, fragmented sequence of *The Little Prince*. The rose. The hat. The baobabs. I roll my eyes when I realize that the Little Prince lives on Asteroid 325. "Of course he does," I whisper to myself.

But the part about the lamplighter hits me in the head like a Frisbee. I hadn't given it much attention during my first read. I read it over again. And then one more time. Some poor fellow who lights his lamp and puts it out over and over because of *orders*. I wonder what it would be like to do the same thing every day again and again with no agency or afterthought. And then I hear those words again: *Daily, how honest have you been since you moved here?*

Plot idea: *Boy discovers that he is, indeed, a work of fiction.*

I'm not sure what Orion has gotten out of his seventy-four reads of *The Little Prince*. But Matthias was right. There's something worth finding tucked away in these pages.

CHAPTER 38

Seascape

WHEN I WOKE UP TODAY, ONE OF THE BURN-
ers in my soul was on low heat. Energy stirring,
pulsing. If I was an inanimate object today, I'd be a time-
bomb, or maybe worse. All through school, my mind races
around the lamplighter, Stormy's challenge of my honesty,
and Lillian's words about needing to accept pain to begin
healing.

I don't have room in my brain for Mr. Tippin's praise
when I turn in my completed reading log for the first time
since February. And there's also no room for Rhett's shining
new cotton candy pink hair, a celebration of his complete
recovery. Though it does look kind of nice.

But none of that today. The heat rises as I practice the
words over and over in my head. It rises as I walk past
Willoughby Lane to the library. It rises during the car ride
home.

And during a brief silence at the dinner table, it all comes to a boil.

"I need to ask a question," I blurt. "It's about Dad. Please let me ask it." Mom and Oakley look to each other and back to me. Neither protests. Not talking about Dad or that night has become our own private family *non*. It always leads to yelling. Or crying. Or something breaking. And often times those things are my fault.

Say it right, Chris, I think. *Just be honest.*

"What's on your mind, Critter?"

The world and all the planets and all the heavenly things in space come to a halt for me. I let the words run free. "Do you ever feel like it was your fault?" I ask, holding back my tears. Neither of them seems surprised by my question.

Somewhere in the sky, a new star is born.

Oakley nods.

"Every day, Critter," Mom says. "Every day."

"Me too," I admit.

Plot idea: *Lamplighter boy abandons his post.*

I tell them that I've been obsessing over it. That I wish I could go back in time and just go downtown with him to watch the Huskies game. That I should've put down the markers. It would have been so easy. Oakley starts to cry into her soup. I tell them that I think about it every time I see our art supplies lying about. Every time I bite my non-painted fingernails. Every time I feel homesick, which is pretty much always. "I'm sorry," I say. "I could have done things different." I exhale, and so much more than air leaves my body. I expected to cry, but somehow, I made it through.

"I wish I didn't have the party," Oakley says. "We were the reason Dad wanted to go." She dries her eyes with her sleeve.

"I wish I wouldn't have let him leave," Mom says. "He must've asked ten times if I was okay with him stepping out. He would have stayed if I had asked." She reaches out for one of my hands and one of Oakley's. "But Fritz kids, listen up." She holds on tight. Really tight. "Nothing that happened that day is your fault. Nothing. Shaun made his own decisions. Unfortunately, he let his fun-loving side cloud his judgement." Her voice gives a quiver. "There are blessings to count, you know. There are others who lost way more than we did that day." Oakley and I nod in unison. "I love him. I miss him. And I know you do, too. But we cannot take responsibility for his decisions."

"Mom?" I ask.

"Yes, sweetheart?"

"Can we put his picture up? Please?"

I wonder a lot about Dad and whether or not he can hear the messages I try transmitting over to him. I wonder if he gets a certain feeling when I'm thinking about him, like the universe is carrying my energy over so he can know. I tuck my thumbs.

I'm sorry, Dad. I tried. I wanted Orion's plan to work. I wanted to leap back to be with you for our trip to Seattle. I wanted to believe that Orion could do it, but I think maybe I always kind of knew. You wouldn't be proud of me, Dad. I've been like the lamplighter lately. Existing with no hope and no purpose. But I'm going to change that now. Which means I have to accept it. I have to accept that you made your own decisions. I'm in Cortland now. And maybe I could have done something different that day. But maybe you could've, too. I love you. I hope you'll come see us here when you can. Transmit back, please.

"Mom? I have another question."

"Okay."

"Will you help me unpack my room tonight?"

And so dinner becomes a move-in circus. Disney songs blast out on a random loop from mom's phone while Oakley teaches the whole town how to sing. My skyline of boxes becomes a landscape, and eventually just a few broken down pieces of cardboard. Oakley says she's going to miss having a hobo for a brother as she helps me put all my shirts on hangers. And within the hour, I'm moved in. Finally. Only took three and a half months.

Mom tries to be sneaky as she takes seven thousand pictures of *Chris's unboxing*. And looking out from my bed, it feels nice to see my art supplies. My bookshelf full with so many stories I had forgotten about, including the still-unfinished *Ranger Oakley vs. The Anti-Green Hobgoblins*. My Seattle Mariners poster. My fluffy reading chair and checkered rug. A box of puzzles and games that Flint and Calvin gave to me.

Mom sneaks out and returns with her hands behind her back. "Critter, only if you're comfortable with it." And she places a framed picture of me and Dad on my desk. "I've been keeping it because I didn't know if you wanted to see it." It's from when we were playing catch in the sand on Whistler Beach. Mom had captured the moment perfectly. It's two mitt-wearing silhouettes against a bright afternoon seascape, baseball soaring left to right. Navy-blue sky, shining green sea. Playing catch, just Dad and me.

I touch the picture and I can feel my soul cry out. Makes me wonder if Orion was actually onto something by using pictures to leap back in time.

"I love it," I say. "Thanks."

Mom and I reminisce about Dad for another hour as we lie together on my bed. We retell the stories. We laugh at the old jokes. I cry a little bit, but Mom cries more. She nods along as I tell her everything Orion had schemed up and how I was planning on leaping back to help Dad. It takes a lot of words to catch her up to speed. "But I don't think he meant any harm," I say.

"That's graceful of you, Critter."

"You know what's cool?" I ask. "He really did invent something marvelous. It just wasn't what I expected. But I think it helped us both," I say. "His world, I mean." Mom's giving me this smile. Like she wants me to do all the talking. Like she's noticing every little particle of me and appreciating every single one. "Mom, he's still not talking. I'm worried about him."

"He's processing. And I'm so proud of you for trying to help him the way you are." I roll over and Mom rubs my back gently. I've missed this. A lot.

"But how long will it take?" I ask.

"Chris, do you think you'll ever forget about what happened with Shaun?" she asks.

"No way!"

"There's no timeline, Critter. He's learning to live with a new weight on his heart. Sort of like you are. And he'll find his way. But he'll never be done remembering, nor will he want to be. Orion will be okay. He just needs more time."

"Are we going to be okay, Mom?"

"I'm sure of it, my dear."

Mom brings me back my navy-blue Mariners hoodie and sets it on my desk chair. "Just in case you want to wear it tonight," she says.

"No thanks, Mom. I'm okay."

CHAPTER 39

Correction

RHETT IS SURPRISINGLY CALM WHEN I TELL him that I'm going to skip the final Junior Surge invitational. I tell him that I'm out of shape after missing ten straight practices. I've missed the morning routines, but I know I'm doing the right thing by skipping. I tell him that somebody needs me here in Cortland right now.

"McBride is lucky to have you, dude," he says with a flip of his pink bangs. I ask him if he's mad about me skipping. "Nah, what you're doing is probably more important," he says. Which I guess is as much sympathy as Rhett's ever going to afford Orion. Now that Rhett has two usable arms again, I don't feel bad about dropping my relay team. I was kind of the substitute anyway.

Instead of swimming, my Saturday is filled with latest Books of The Day: *Third Graders in Space* and *The Day the Johnson Boys Moved In*. The first book is fast and easy. But the second one is hard because I can feel my voice starting to peter out. I've probably said more words in the last week than I have in the last year.

Sunday, I return with cough drops and a new book, *Back Before Sunrise*. Orion must not love fantasy because he's already asleep and I'm only on chapter three. I miss his voice. And his sunny smile. I wonder about vocal chords. How mine are tired from too much talking. How his are probably rusty from not talking enough. He's got something on his face that looks like syrup as he drifts into the heavy, real part of sleep. Good to know he's eating, at least.

It took some weekend begging, but Mom lets me stay home from school today. She says she'll be disappointed if I am trying to get out of an assignment or deadline for Mr. Tippin, but I assure her that I simply have a responsibility to Orion right now. "Just this one day, Critter." And so I load up my backpack with picture books from both Oakley's shelves and the library and sit close enough for Orion to see every detail. Every book holds his attention thoroughly. Reading all of these picture books only supercharges my desire to make my own. I daydream about what stories I want to tell as I rest my voice from Orion's purple bean bag.

"I reread your book," I say, mostly to myself. "I've been thinking about it a lot lately. About the characters and what they say." Orion reaches for his own copy of *The Little Prince* on his nightstand and holds it with two hands. "I don't think I was paying attention to the right stuff the first time," I tell him. "But when I read it again, so much more made sense. Like what the kid is doing and why, I think. And I think about that thing the fox said a lot. How we can't see the important stuff, or something like that." Orion coughs.

And coughs again.

And he sits up on his bed.

And he clears his throat.

"That's not how the quote goes," he says.

CHAPTER 40

Voyage

ORION HUGS TIGHT. AND I HUG TIGHT BACK. AND I don't know what to say because I don't want him to slip back into silence. I don't want to say the wrong thing.

My brain goes back to the day we met. We're two boys in a heap on the ground again and I still don't know what to say. But, as usual, Orion beats me to it.

"You know that star?" he asks, still holding on. He coughs away his vocal rust. "The one you got me for my birthday?" I tell him yes. "I look for it every night." He looks like he might start crying. "He said he's going to go exploring there, and that's where I'd be able to find him." And then the tears start to come.

"I'm sorry, Orion."

"I'm sorry I got your hopes up," he says. "You were the only one in town who didn't know. I needed to get away from it."

"It was nice to dream," I say. He stands up and grabs his red photo journal from his nightstand. Hiding in the pages is a familiar-looking index card.

"He gave me one last mission before he left." And written in thin marker lines is: *Never let the Light of Orion fade.* He brushes his finger over the writing and holds the card close to his chest.

"Sounds like we have a lot more pictures to take then," I say. And there it is. That cartoony smile.

"Thanks, Christopher Fritz. For everything. I hope you're not mad."

"I'm not mad. But I do have a question." I wonder if it's the wrong time to ask. But it's been a fly in my brain ever since Lillian called me over to talk. So much of Orion's story could be explained away. Room 325. The missions. The leaping. The key. There's one piece of the puzzle I just haven't been able to find. Right time or not, I'm unsure. But my heart needs to ask. "How did you know my name the day we met?"

Orion smiles and nods. "I'll show you." He slips into his desk chair and opens his laptop. A few keystrokes and clicks later, he stands up and pushes me in the chair with two hands. "Read," he says.

The screen is grey and pink. At the top there is a wide picture of me and Oakley standing between Mom and Dad. It's the fall picture we took a few years ago. The banner says in swirly font: THE FRITZ FAMILY VOYAGE. "What is this?" I ask.

"Your mom writes about you. A lot," Orion says. "I was bored one day during my suspension and I read the article on Cortland News about the new photography teacher coming in. I searched her up, found this, and I noticed the picture of your new house right away. Right next to mine. I got really curious about you guys and I read every single word."

There are thousands of words. Tens of thousands. And so many pictures. There's the one Mom took from the kitchen after Oakley's music lesson. And there's my pictures with Rhett before practice, and more of us at the invitational. Oakley and her teacher. Oakley and Kadence. Every now and then there is one of Dad. And so many words.

Plot idea: *Zookeeper boy discovers he is actually part of the exhibit.*

I had no idea Mom was keeping her thoughts in a place like this for everybody to see. I guess she does always have that tablet in her hands. It makes sense. And then one picture catches my eye. It's of me. It's black and white and I'm sitting crisscross in the middle of Willoughby Lane. "That's the day we met!" I say. It surprises me that Mom saw me sitting there and didn't lecture me about it.

"Read it," Orion says. I scroll up to the top of the post.

· · · · ·

Sing, Sweet Songbird, Sing.

I see you, my Songbird. I see you. And I want to hear you.

Your spirit longs for home. Your heart longs for family.

Your poor wings clipped by forces far outside your reach.

I'm sorry, sweet Songbird.

Let me help you fly.

Let me help you sing.

Please

~

Christopher isn't okay. To say that his spirit is shattered right now would be an understatement. He's gone quiet ever since we sold the house. He's walking in a daydream that he won't wake up from.

I keep telling myself that he'll wake up when he's ready. But it breaks this mama's heart to see her vibrant and cheerful son fall into this malaise. I wish I could carry his pain for him. I would give anything to hear his hum and chirp like when he draws and writes with Spiral. His shine is gone. I want to give him his peace back. His peace that was so unfairly taken from him. What I wouldn't give right now.

Being a mama has introduced me to so many joys and wonders that I never could have imagined. It's my life's only calling. But it also has shown me a new level of heartbreak and pain. Seeing Critter like this hurts. Send those extra prayers if you have them, my friends. We've just crash landed in Cortland and I think we're in critical condition.

. . . . .

Mom's been with me the whole time. She was the first one to hold me after Dad's accident. And she's the one with me now, helping make the best of things here. It makes me sad to know how I made her feel. But there's something I feel that is shining brighter than the sadness as I read Mom's words. It's love. More of it than I can stand. I explore deeper into this wordy world Mom has kept hidden from us.

There's a post about me and my swimming. Mom thinks that I'm trying to *muscle up* because she suspects there is somebody I'm trying to impress. Her writing is vague, but I know who she's talking about. I can feel my face heat up because I remember that Orion suspected the same thing, hence his letter.

And maybe they're right. Maybe not. I'm not totally sure. But that's for later.

Scrolling through all of this writing makes me feel like Mom has discovered her own way of going back in time, too. There's a post about Oakley and how Mom is worried about her behavior at school. Crying, tantrums, defiance. Classic Oakley. Another from a few months ago about how Mom is going to look into library hours because *she is desperate for afterschool options.* Another from the day before that about Mom hoping that her kids' new teachers were as good as the previous ones. Orion sure had me figured out before even I had me figured out.

One post is simply a link to Dad's article. That one got a

lot of attention. I can't bring myself to click it. Not yet.

"There's so much here," I say.

"I sometimes felt guilty when I read this stuff," Orion says. "I checked back a lot to see what she had written. I'm sorry for not telling you the truth. I feel bad about it."

"That's because you're a really big *heart person*, Orion." He gasps. "You know that's not a bad thing, right?"

He pushes me out of the chair. "Shut your big stupid mouth, Christopher Fritz."

And we laugh and we laugh.

CHAPTER 41

Dessert

MY WALK HOME TODAY IS QUICK. I WANT TO see Orion. Maybe he'll have gotten dressed and be ready for me. I want Stormy to see him. Or at the very least, tell Stormy about yesterday. If I was an animal today, I'd be a rabbit winning in a game of tag. I skip over every crack in the sidewalk as I bounce my way to Willoughby Lane.

There's no Orion. But Mom's car sits whirring in the driveway and she's waving me over. Big grin.

"Critter! Let's go get your sister!"

"What's going on? Why are you home so early?"

"I want to celebrate a great day with my great kids. Get in, we're going for a treat." I guess Orion will have to wait a while. He'd understand.

We snag Oakley from the Weston afterschool program and zip over to Ramsey's. It's a local dessert shop that

Oakley's been dying to try out, but Mom always said that winter is no time for ice cream. Or that she's too tired after work. There's always something. But Oakley nearly bursts a blood vessel when she opens the menu and sees her many options.

It's chocolate cheesecake for me. Mine and Dad's favorite. Oakley goes for a waffle brownie sundae, which might hold the world record for being the most sugary thing ever invented. "Hey!" Oakley says as Mom steals a bite. "You said you weren't hungry!"

"Tough luck, kiddo," Mom teases as she steals another. Mom sure is glowing today. I'm used to seeing too-tired-to-talk Mom at dinner time. She's reminding me of Mom from Oregon. Mom from before the emergency. Stormy said that we're all our own main characters. And after reading what she's been writing about online, I've been wondering about what cosmic transmissions has she been sending out. To Dad? To me?

"Okay you two," Mom says. "I have news."

"What's up?" I ask.

"Honesty time. How are you two liking Cortland?" Oakley and I trade glances.

Oakley goes first. "I like it here," she says. "I love my teacher. And Kadence is pretty much my best friend ever." Mom nods.

"Critter?"

My brain lags out when she asks me directly. I've over-spent my energy trying to get out of Cortland over the past several months. I've been trying to escape to a different timeline altogether. But my heart is singing something new today that I can't ignore: I've really enjoyed my time with Orion. And my talks and book conversations with Stormy. And joining the Junior Surge with Rhett.

"Well," I say, "I think I like it a lot more than I thought I would. I like the people I've met."

Mom is grinning a mighty grin. "I'm glad to hear that," she says. "Because today I was offered a full-time position for next school year. An actual teacher contract." My heart goes double-time. "I want to take it. But I wanted to check in with you two first. I wanted to see if we were all comfortable making Cortland our home permanently."

This time, it's easy. The words line themselves up perfectly in my head.

"Take the job, Mom," I say.

"Yes! Take it!" Oakley adds. Weight vanishes from Mom's shoulders and face as she holds her hands prayer style and mouths *thank you.*

Plot idea: *Boy soldier seeks to raze village, ends up moving in.*

I like it when the sun sets later and later. When there's more time in the evenings to go outside, even if it's just to sit in the grass to drift and daydream. Orion is lying flat on his back in my front yard. White shorts today. "I'm packing up my stuff soon," he says. "I'm moving across town."

"You better come back," I say. "We have missions to do." And he assures me that I'll never be able to get rid of him.

Mom steps out into the evening air with her phone in her hand.

"Critter," she says. "Your Dad's on the phone. Would you like to talk to him?" My joints go stiff and I forget to breathe. My brain overloads with words like it always does and I can feel my blood move faster through me. Orion's looking at me. Mom's looking at me. Somewhere under this beautiful spring sky, Dad is waiting.

I take the phone from Mom's hand and my mouth goes dry. And I want to scream. I want to cry. I want to tell him off for the decisions he made in Oregon. I want to tell him that he wasn't there for my third-place finish. And he wasn't there for Matthias's funeral. And that I still want to see a Mariners game this summer. But a single wave washes away those thoughts and leaves behind something clearer. "Hi, Dad," I say.

And the words line themselves up perfectly in my head. They are the only words my heart has. And they are essential: "I miss you."

CHAPTER 42

Apology Not Accepted

MY LAST WEEK AS AN ELEMENTARY SCHOOL student feels very *final*. Mr. Tippin won't stop talking about the grit and resolve we demonstrated this year, and how he's excited to launch *such an extraordinary class of leaders into CMS.* I have to admit, I feel proud to have finally been awarded leader of the week. It may have taken until the end of May, but it really does mean something. Mr. Tippin takes that award as seriously as Orion does make-believe.

The entire fifth grade class piles onto a bus to visit Cortland Middle School. Sixth grader "guides" who used to go to Weston Elementary greet us in the cafeteria, which is probably three times bigger than ours *and* has a salad bar. I watch my classmates reunite with their sixth-grade friends. High fives, playful shoves. Makes me think of Orion next year. He won't be going to Weston anymore, but maybe they'll let me be a guide for him anyway.

Rhett introduces me to a tall, lean boy named Logan, who clearly isn't impressed by Rhett's hair. "I love the pink, Sprinkles," he jabs at Rhett. But Rhett takes it all in stride.

He tells me that Logan is the one who first convinced him to join the Junior Surge. "Fritzy here joined up this winter, and I think he's going to stick with us next year, right?" Rhett asks as he slaps my back. "Next year, the real competition starts."

There's something about Rhett that I just can't say no to. "Yeah, I'll probably do it," I say. Rhett whoops loud enough for every classroom to hear as we make our way upstairs to learn how to use the lockers.

On the bus ride back, Ava hands me a piece of paper that is closed with tape. It has *Orion* written in red marker. The two have been writing letters back and forth for days, and I've been stuck delivering them. I can still hear the accent Orion used when he said, "Be my courier, Christopher Fritz! Stamps are expensive!" I had to look up the word *courier* that night. I'm wicked curious what the letters say, but I've already breached that line once. Never again. Ava and Orion have tamed each other, too, and I can appreciate that.

When I get to the Cortland Community Library, Stormy already has the Book of the Day checked out for me. Her candy jar is open, and I collect my newly instated Chris Tax.

"Stormy, I don't think I'll be coming here very much after school lets out."

"Shucks, Daily. Why might that be?"

"Mom said that next year I can have my own key to the house because I'll be in middle school. And the middle school isn't in walking distance."

Stormy says that makes sense and that it sounds like a new chapter in the story I'm writing about myself. "But I want to read that chapter, Daily, so don't be a stranger," she says. "Come back in a few years and apply. We'll pay you in money instead of candy." We share a laugh. I tuck that thought away in my brain because it actually sounds like something I'd really enjoy. I bet Orion would, too. Which reminds me of Room 325. The hallway and staircase that leads to the old side of the building have been blocked off with caution tape ever since Orion nearly lost his arms.

"Hey, Stormy. What's going to happen with the old offices and stuff?"

"Well, we can't risk any more children mutilating themselves," she says sarcastically. "They're going to be re-purposed."

"Meaning what?" I ask.

"Instead of empty offices and storage closets, the board is going to look into funding a teen section. We'll take out some of those walls and add more middle grade books, computers, couches. For those kids who may have outgrown my domain here," she says with a wink. "Which is complete absurdity."

"That sounds awesome," I say.

"But it'll take some time, Daily. Fundraising, designing. Probably two or three years." I smile. Maybe Orion and I will be getting our space back after all. Maybe we'll be the first teenagers to get to use it.

At home, Oakley sits by me in the grass. I think she knows what she's doing. She knows I won't cry as easily if she's around. And watching Orion load the last of his things into Lillian's black car gets me darn close. I've been counting down the days to Orion's official move, but it still crept up on me fast. Like, way too fast.

We've been spending a lot of time in his room so he could enjoy it for a little longer. Sometimes the tears hit him hard and fast. His father's essence is everywhere. But I get it. I have some of those moments, too. He always says sorry as he fights away the tears, but I will never accept the apology. Loving someone isn't something to be sorry for.

After tossing his astronaut backpack onto the front seat, Orion meets me in the grass. Black shorts. Golden scarf. He pulls me to my feet and offers me a handshake. Tackling, sure. Hugging, sure. But I don't think I've ever shaken hands with Orion before. "I'm not saying bye to you," he says.

"Fine," I say with a playful shove. He smiles and I see something in his eyes. No wild horses. No raging storm. If Mom was standing with me, I think she'd say it's what peace looks like. And I think she'd be right.

"See you soon," he says. He gallops over to the passenger

side and doesn't even see me waving as Lillian puts the car in reverse and steers outward, onward, and away.

There he goes. My cartoon neighbor; the fifth grader who can't tie shoes; the best pretender in the history of kids; the boy from Willoughby Lane no longer; my best friend, Orion McBride. Without him, I'm not sure I would have ever left my bedroom. Maybe I would have flunked out of Weston Elementary. Maybe I would have begged Mom to not take the job. Maybe.

But here I am. I'm glad he dragged me into his world without asking for permission. And after all these months, I still can't figure out what it is. He's just got a sunshine about him. And I'm not going to spend any more energy wondering about how or why. Because to me, he's unique in all the world.

CHAPTER 43

Summer

H I, DAD. I'VE BEEN THINKING ABOUT YOU A lot lately. *Today's the day we would have been in Seattle. Playing catch by myself isn't quite what I had in mind. But it's still time with you, so I guess I'll take it. I hope you get to see Cortland someday. I don't know if I'll still be here when you have that chance, but it's so pretty in the summertime. The way the whole town blooms and glows. The way those mountains cast their mighty shadows. I wanted to hate it here. But Orion made that impossible. I hope you get the chance to meet him, too. He's weird. You'd love him.*

I still feel sad about it sometimes, Dad. I still feel like I could have done things differently. But I know what makes the desert beautiful is that somewhere it hides a well. That's what the Little Prince taught me. I'm learning to take the pen for myself and own my decisions. I'm sorry I gave up on the leap. But I wonder if this is what you'd want from me. It's taken some time and a whole lot of aching, but I think I'm going to be okay.

"Christopher Fritz!" My baseball nearly bonks my head as I look in the direction of the shout. Orion yells my name again as he swerves around the corner and pedals his wobbly self up to my yard. His inky black helmet matches his new, glossy bike.

"Baseball's over," he says. "We have a mission. Now." He points to his astronaut backpack with his Polaroid camera sticking out of the top.

"Where are we going?" I ask.

"You'll see when we get there. Ava's waiting. Let's go!" And he's off. A trail of sunshine for me to follow down Willoughby Lane. I pick up my bike off the grass and I'm right behind him.

And that's the truth, Dad. I'm learning to live with the ache. I think we all are.

And we're going to be okay.

Acknowledgements

LIKE CHRISTOPHER FRITZ, I OWE MUCH OF THE success of this journey to the clever and relentlessly supportive people that surround me.

To my professional teammates David Miles and Claire Evans—how can I thank you enough for the attention, love, and professionalism you've shown this project? David, your artistic vision and touch has brought Christopher and Orion's journey to life with such gentle and sincere flair, true to their personalities! From cover to cover and everything in between, thank you for everything. And Claire, your keen eye, attention to every detail, and thorough question asking has helped the text become its best-possible self. I am so grateful for the dedication and energy you've both contributed to this story. My sincerest thanks to you both.

To Grandma Chris, one of the very best people in the world to discuss writing and story ideas with. Thank you so much for believing in me and in this story. From before I ever wrote the first word all the way through many completed drafts, your encouragement and passion for fiction helped this story find its wings.

A mighty big thank you to Viktor Kapiliovich, a true friend and enthusiastic supporter of both me and this project. Your contribution to this story's success is so appreciated. Next time Libera comes around, dinner is on me.

To my fantastic beta team—Emily, Erica, Joss, Noah, Lydia, Rachael, Sydney, and Cassidy—thank you for taking a risk on a new story from a newbie author. Our honest conversations about Christopher, Orion, their arcs, their aches, and everything else in Cortland helped develop the story at every turn. Each of you contributed feedback that now lives within the text. Thank you for your support. I owe you all tacos!

To the Scriveners: Mac'n Scriv for LIFE!

Finally, a sincere thank you to every student I have had the chance to work with since the start of my wonderful teaching career, and even to those who I have yet to meet. Much like Christopher Fritz, the things that are essential in my life are held up by two pillars: meaning and connection. Being a teacher provides my soul with all the meaning and connection I could ever hope for, and I owe so much of who I am to my time spent in the classroom with you. Let's keep doing really big, really awesome things together.

CPSIA information can be obtained
at www.ICGtesting.com
Printed in the USA
FSHW011011030321
79138FS